TRISTAN

LEANN ASHERS

Tristan

Cover Designer: Regina Wamba
Photographer: Wander Aguiar
Editor: Courtney Delollis
Editor: Virginia Tesi Carey
Formatter: HJ Bellus

PROLOGUE

LYNN

Thirteen Years Old

I PRETEND I don't hear the footsteps thundering up the hallway toward my bedroom.

My fists clench onto my threadbare blanket that is so old that it doesn't even provide any kind of warmth anymore.

This scene is all too familiar. I remember the morning that they wrenched open Etta's bedroom door, tore her from her bed to marry someone twice her age.

Once, I saw my mother and father talking in secret in the kitchen, but they stopped the second I walked into the room. I knew it would soon be time for it to happen to me and I have dreaded that day ever since.

In our church, their beliefs are that at the age of thirteen, girls and boys are considered an adult and they are of age to marry. However, for girls, it's a fear that we all face and not something to look forward to.

The day I turned thirteen, my life as I knew it was gone. My worst fear came to life.

I knew my time was up. I hold my breath listening and praying that they walk past my room to another part of the house. I can see their footsteps outside of the door and my heart sinks when two more sets of feet join them.

Fear unlike I have ever felt before hits me. My bedroom door opens and standing at the entrance are my father Michael and an older man I have never seen before.

My father walks into the room, his hands large, demanding as he reaches down and grabs me by my arms, dragging me out of bed.

I wince at his tight fist gripping me. "Ow," I hiss and my father's eyes glare at me with pure hatred.

I look over at the man who supposedly is my new husband, who appears to be around the same age as my father. I try not to throw up at the thought of what is going to happen to me, what I will have to suffer for the rest of my life.

Living with my parents has been hell, but the look in his eyes tells me this is going to be worse than anything I have ever imagined. I'd rather die.

"Come on my darlin, it's time to take you home." He grins at me, showing his very crooked teeth. He takes my hand, wrenching me against his chest.

"We have a busy day ahead of us."

My life as I knew it was over. And a new kind of hell has begun.

1

LYNN

AGE TWENTY-ONE

I smile at Michaela over my cup of coffee. Her hair is a mess from where she rolls around in her sleep and most of the time ends up on the floor, so I stick pillows by her bed just to be on the safe side.

My sweet angel is seven years old. I had her when I was only fourteen years old, still a baby myself. But she is the best thing that has graced my life so far.

She smiles at me, her eyes sleepy. Suddenly, her eyes pop open and her smile turns into a wide grin, showing her missing two front teeth. "Is that bacon I smell?" she asks.

I nod laughing. "Along with some French toast. Dig in, sweet girl." I help her sit down and hand her her plate. I kiss the top of her head; I love her so much.

Every day I thank God that she doesn't have to live the life that I did growing up. I sit down beside her talking to her about school and how she wants to play softball with Tiffany, Lane and Amelia's daughter.

I push her hair over her shoulder so she doesn't get syrup in it. "Can I wear my new jeans today, Mommy?" she asks between syrupy bites.

"You can, baby. I also packed you an extra sandwich liked you asked for your friend too." She grins happily at that.

One of her friends forgot their lunch once and it devastated her, so she has decided that she must bring extras in case that ever happens again. My precious angel.

"Alright, go get dressed," I urge her and she runs upstairs to her room. I put the plate in the dishwasher.

I pull out my briefcase and look over my first client of the day's file so I can prepare myself; it's a four-year-old little girl.

I am a therapist who specializes in trauma, mostly PTSD. Working with kids is hard on me mentally, but I know therapy is so important when it comes to your healing journey.

I know if my brother didn't get me into therapy as soon as he rescued me from the cult, I wouldn't have recovered like I did. I am forever thankful for that.

Michaela runs down the stairs making one final jump at the bottom of the stairs with her backpack on her. "Ready, Mom!" She does a little twirl showing me her new jeans and Converse shoes.

"Wow, you're so beautiful, my angel." I walk over and smoosh her cheeks together giving her a kiss. She giggles trying to get away. "Mommy!" she squeals and runs to the front door.

The sound of her laughter makes me so happy. I will never forget the second I laid eyes on her and the love I had for her, how much I wanted to protect her.

Etta and I made it our mission to get out and find our brothers. I didn't want Michaela to suffer the same fate as us and so many other women.

"Mom, I have softball practice after school today," Michaela reminds me as I buckle her in her booster seat.

"I remember and I'm to bring the cookies, right?"

Her eyes light up. "You got it, dude." She lifts her hand with her thumb up like Michelle from *Full House*, her favorite show.

ETTA IS WAITING for me outside of the compound. I have my own office inside of the compound where we bring all of the women that are brought from cults and other horrible situations. It's basically a huge house with a lot of rooms. Once the girls are stable, we transfer them to another house on the property where they live as long as they want.

Etta has on her gear letting me know that she is going on a mission. Etta is the one that goes on the front line and fights to get them out. I fight for their mental health; I am their shoulder to lean on.

"Who are you going after today?" I ask, setting my bag on the steps.

Her face is serious as she is deep in thought, I know she is preparing herself. "She is a single mom of two kids, both under the age of five and she is only seventeen."

Fuck! A cold chill runs down my body. I was forced to marry at thirteen, but it's different hearing about others suffering the same fate. Believe it or not, we have rescued some younger than I was when I married.

"I have Michaela's game later but once it's over I will come back here to wait on you guys to get back." I walk over and hug her tightly. I am terrified as I watch her leave.

But this is what we are meant to do, this is our lives. We got a second chance at life and we want others to have that too.

An SUV pulls down the huge driveway and I can see my brother and Trey in the front seat, one of them always goes with Etta to make sure she is safe.

"Hi, Lynn." Trey gets out first and pulls me into a hug. Etta and I have gotten really close with Trey over the years.

"Hi, Trey. How are the twins?" I ask, patting his back before pulling my brother into a hug.

Vinny smiles widely at the mention of his, Trey, and Lani's

kids. "They are getting bigger every single day and it's breaking our hearts."

My heart swells with the love I have for Caleb and Sariah. "Michaela gets more independent every day and it hurts my heart."

"So, which one of you guys are going with Etta?" I ask.

Vinny lifts his hand and Trey smiles at me. "That means I get to see Michaela's game today and next time it's Vinny."

"She will be so excited! Now I have to bake some cookies to take tonight." I pick up my case and make my way inside of the compound to put on the cookies before my first client.

MICHAELA IS in the middle of the field warming up talking to Tiffany who is a legend around here when it comes to softball.

I set the huge platter of cookies on the table where they have the drinks lined up. Grace, who is Aiden's ole lady, he is a member of the Grim Sinners MC with Lane, Tiffany's dad, smiles at me when I drop them off. "How are you doing, girl?" I ask.

She smiles happily and looks over at Aiden who is watching her like a hawk. "I'm good, how are you?"

I pat her back. "I'm good, ready to see my girl play."

Grace looks at Michaela. "She is really good. Honestly, Tiffany better be careful because Michaela can sneak up on her in a few years."

I laugh at that. "She is obsessed, that is for sure." I love that she is passionate about something, she has been since the moment she came to Tiffany's game years ago.

"How is she doing?" Trey says out of nowhere scaring the piss out of me. I turn around glaring at him and he has a shit-eating grin on his face letting me know that he did it on purpose.

6

Michaela looks over at us suddenly, waving excitedly. This is her first game: they have been practicing for months.

I wave back and she jumps up and down, my baby has grown up. She looks so cute in her little softball uniform with the bow in her hair.

"I am going to go find myself a seat," I tell Grace and I find an empty bleacher behind our dugout and Aiden joins me sitting beside me with Trey on the other side. Leah passes by us, waving and running onto the field to join Tiffany. Leah, who is Aiden and Grace's adopted daughter, is just as talented as Tiffany and together they are a force to be reckoned with.

"I can't believe my baby is a fucking teenager now," Aiden grumbles, watching her run onto the field. He looks devastated.

I pat his shoulder. "She is a good kid though," I point out.

He grins at that. "She gets that from her mom for sure."

I swoon at that. Soon the stands fill with people. The girls run to the dugout to wait for the game to start and have the Grace pep talk.

"I think this game is going to be a piece of cake. Look how small all of those runts are."

My eyes narrow at the person's words behind me. I don't turn around and glare, as much as I am itching to do so. Trey cringes beside me and I wiggle my toes in my shoes trying to chill myself out.

The game starts and the commenter behind me is totally forgotten. "Go, baby!" I yell at Michaela who is going to be second at bat.

Leah and Tiffany are standing beside Grace helping coach the girls. Michaela is second up at bat and I am nervous for her; I want her to hit it so bad.

The first girl tapped the ball and barely made it to first base. I hold my breath when Michaela lifts her bat and nods.

"Come on. Come on." I grip Trey's forearm and pray.

Swing. "Strike one!"

I am dying, my heart is slowly stopping. Some of the fuckers behind me are laughing but right now Michaela is what's important.

Michaela closes her eyes and I know she is collecting herself.

"You got this, baby," I say under my breath.

WHACK.

I stand up, jumping up and down when the ball soars to the outfield. "GO! GO! GO!" I swing my arms like a loon and move to the fence to get a closer look as she makes it to second base and the first batter on the third.

Michaela is grinning ear to ear so proud of herself and I want to cry for my baby. I turn around and look at Trey who is looking thrilled too.

Aiden is laughing at me being ridiculous. I point at him, "Don't forget how you've gotten torn up from the floor from Leah."

He quits laughing but that doesn't hide the amusement in his eyes. I sit back down with a happy sigh. This is all that she wanted, to hit the ball.

"Fucking parents," one of the women behind me mutters and I bite my lip nodding to myself to keep my cool because this is about the kids and not this hoe behind me.

I let out a deep breath and I see Trey eyeing me to the side but I ignore him too. It doesn't slip past me that Michaela continues to look over at me to make sure I am watching her and she will get my full attention, bitches be damned.

The next girl hits the ball easily and the third base runs home. Michaela is looking behind her and she rounds third base and I hold my breath hoping she makes to home plate.

She slides into home, her fingers barely touching the plate when the girl catches the ball. "Go, baby!" I scream and she stands up jumping, so excited.

I run to the fence not even caring if I am being dramatic. It's where she gets it from. "Mommy did you see me!" She grins with her teeth missing.

God, I love my sweet baby.

"Yes sweetheart, I am so proud of you!" I stick my hand through the fence and touch her face before she runs to the dugout where the girls are singing.

I sit back down and laugh to myself at the girls, they are such great kids and so supportive of each other.

I ignore the whispering behind me but I catch a few words. "She is so young."

I've heard that so many times. Yes, I am twenty-one years old with a seven-year-old, but that doesn't change the fact I am a good ass mom.

The game passes by in a blur, the other team not even scoring. We won by a landslide.

I stand by the entrance of the field with Trey waiting for Michaela to come out with the girls.

"This shit was rigged. I bet she's fucking the umpires." I turn around at that and come face to face with the woman who has smarted off to me all night.

Her face shows her shock knowing that I have caught her. "Look, if you're jealous just say so. No point in being a bitch." I smile sweetly and turn back around not giving her another ounce of my time.

Trey bursts out laughing. I'm not someone who will confront another person. I'm a lover not a fighter, but a person can only handle so much.

"Well, I am happy to see the mean side to Lynn, I missed it," Trey jokes and bops me on the head.

I roll my eyes and Michaela runs through the gate, straight to me. "Mom I did so good! Tiffany and Leah said so!" She hugs me, jumping side to side, laughing.

I lean back slightly so I can see her face. "I am so incredibly

9

proud of you sweeheart, you have worked so hard and you did so great today!" I congratulate her.

She smiles back at me so beautifully. "I love you, Mom." She hugs me tightly and I hug her back. Trey rubs the back of her head and she turns to him. "Trey!" she squeals. He picks her up off the ground and hugs her. "Hi, squirt."

"Mom, can we get pizza for dinner?"

"That works, honey, I don't feel like cooking anyway," I admit. Today has me drained mentally as I had some hard cases today.

"I will follow you guys home to make sure you make it," Trey tells us. I thank him as he walks us to our car.

I keep an eye out for the crazy mother. I have seen the worst of society and I don't put anything past anyone. People are crazy.

I put Michaela in her seat, watching to make sure she buckles before I shut the door. I click the key fob to lock the door, then manually open my door. I know that's probably overkill, but no one is taking my kid.

We wave bye to Trey after pulling into our yard, the gate shutting behind us. I live on the compound property but I have my own driveway and house away from everyone.

"Come on Mom, waiting for this pizza is killing me," Michaela groans, half-starved.

Tristan

WE BOARD the helicopter that is picking us up in the middle of the desert; we just completed our last mission and I am retiring from the SEALs.

I have seen so many horrible things, things that would forever fuck with my mind but I would do it all over again to protect my country.

One thing that stuck with me through it all was a kid who wore a bomb strapped to his chest, injuring one of my friends that I went through basics with.

That shit sticks with you.

We have slept on the ground, on the sand many fucking nights where the temperature drops below freezing once it gets dark with the enemy right over the hill.

We have been deployed for a year and we have been all over the middle eastern countries on missions.

But I am ready to be with my family, I am ready to be a full-time member of my MC and take my place as enforcer.

I look at my brothers on the helicopter with me. We all have mixed feelings about joining the civilian life full-time but we need this, we have sacrificed so much to protect our country. It's time to hand over the reins.

"Come join the MC guys with me," I ask them once more, they are all thinking about it and I know that they will all follow me. I have talked about my MC for the last year with them.

Darren nods. "I am with you, brother."

Most of them don't have any family and if they do, they aren't close, none of them are married or have kids. Joining the MC gives you that brotherhood that you have in the military.

I already cleared it with my brothers for them to prospect if they decide to join.

I look at the ground below me, the desert looking more and more menacing the further we are from it. The land stretching out for miles, lifeless, and the heat you can never escape. It's hell.

First things fucking first, I am going to get me a huge ass burger and collapse into bed for days. We have been living off MRES for weeks, you can only have spaghetti so many times and fuck plain water, I am over that too. I need a fucking beer.

But most of all, I am ready to go home.

2

LYNN

HOURS LATER

I STAND at the entrance to the main house on the compound, Etta will be here any minute with the girl they rescued earlier today.

Etta texted me on the way over that she is really struggling mentally, so I am waiting anxiously.

Michaela is fast asleep in bed and Cindy, one of the women that we took in years ago from a cult in Colorado, is babysitting her until I get back home.

She can't have kids so she soaks in all of the kid time she can get, which breaks my heart for her.

Lights shine on the driveway letting me know that they are pulling in. Candace, our house mom, walks out of the kitchen staring out of the window with me.

They pull to a stop and I open the front door. Etta jumps out of the back seat holding a young girl that can't even be a teenager yet.

She is sobbing uncontrollably, every sound wrecking a part of my heart. Candace turns her head away and grabs a blanket off the back of one of the couches.

We wait for them to bring her up the stairs and into the

house. "Hi, sweetheart," I say softly. I take the blanket from Candace and wrap it around her shoulders hoping that it brings her some comfort.

She looks at me, her eyes filled with tears, and I can see the pain burrowed deep. The faces of these women will never leave me.

"My name is Lynn; you are safe here." I smile gently. She looks around the house taking everything in.

She is dressed in a white gown, her hair braided down her back. "I'm Rosie."

"It's nice to meet you, sweetheart. I'm going to show you to your room." I lead her up the stairs, tears streaming down her face, her lips trembling with probably fear and I know this is so overwhelming for her.

I push open her bedroom door. "This is my room?" she asks, her voice barely audible from crying so much.

I open her bathroom door and turn on the light so she can see inside. "This is all yours, this is your bathroom." I point inside.

She sits down onto the bed, curling the blanket tighter around her, looking around the room.

"I'm scared, but I would rather be here than back there," she confesses, her face falls looking down onto the floor.

I sit down beside her. "I was raised in a cult just like you were, I remember when I left and how terrified I was. I promise you, one day, it won't be always like this," I reassure her.

She focuses her haunting brown eyes on me. "Are you sure?"

I put my hand on her shoulder. "One day it will be easier, I promise you that." She gives me a slight smile, sniffing and wiping away her tears.

"Pajamas are in your dresser, towels are under the sink. Make yourself at home. If you need anyone Candace is right down the hall. She has a sign outside her door and I will speak

LEANN ASHERS

more with you tomorrow." I slowly shut the door behind me gently, as to not make any loud sounds.

Sometimes the best thing you can do is just let them have privacy and come to terms with their new life. They crave getting away so bad and when they finally do, it takes a bit to hit home.

Life is so much different outside of the cults. In a cult, your whole life is completely controlled, from what time you get up to the color of clothes you wear. Everything.

I walk down the stairs and Etta is in the main room talking to Vinny. Both turn to look at me. "How is she?" Etta asks.

I wave my hand side to side. "It's going to take her awhile to get used to things, especially since she is so young. How old is she anyway?" I ask.

Etta's face drops. "She is twelve." Vinny's jaw clenches and he turns to look out the window.

My stomach drops to my feet at that, just five years older than Michaela and even younger than Leah and Tiffany.

"I'm going to head home to Michaela, I will be back in the morning to begin her first session." I hug Etta and Vinny, both of them are exhausted.

Sometimes I don't know how Etta can do it, she is going straight into the hornet's nest, coming face to face with these people and I know it has to be painful for her. Maybe I need to sit down and talk with her soon, to make sure she is doing okay.

The drive home is short. Cindy is on the couch reading a book when I walk inside. "Hi, Cindy! How are you?" I ask her.

She smiles walking to the front door. "I'm good, she was an angel like usual." She has a wishful look on her face.

"Want to sit down with me?" I ask her, I've been wanting to speak with her about something.

She gives me a confused look but does as I ask. I pat the seat beside me. "Do you know one of the new girls, Rhonda?"

She nods, "Yes, she has the newborn baby."

14

I take her hand. "She is very young, thirteen years old, and she expressed to me a few days ago that she is not sure she is ready to be a mother. She asked if someone could adopt her baby."

Cindy looks at me in shock as it slowly sinks in what I am asking. "Do you mean?" She shakes her head. "Are you saying what I think you are?" she whispers.

I squeeze her hand. "I know you have wanted to be a mother for a while Cindy, you would be the best mother to this sweet baby."

Her eyes fill with tears, she bends her head sobbing. "I have wanted this for so long." She sobs between breaths.

"How about tomorrow we go out shopping, set up your new home, and we can get the paperwork started before we can go and get her?" I suggest.

She wraps her arms around me tightly, squeezing me. "Thank you, thank you!" she whispers over and over. "I will be here as soon as you're back from taking Michaela to school."

"Deal!" I am so excited for her. I am saddened for the mother but mentally she can't care for her child, it was a hard decision for her but it's the best one.

Cindy leaves and I lock the door behind her. I go and push open Michaela's door taking a peek at her to make sure that she is fine.

The sight of her so peaceful in her sleep, warms my heart. I sneak over and press a kiss to the top of her head. I would do anything to protect her, to give her the best life.

I WAKE up to small little feet walking into my bedroom, but I pretend to be asleep to see what she's going to do.

I feel her breath on my face. It takes everything in me not to smile as she studies me, then I feel a little finger touching my nose.

She giggles, then I hear a smacking sound as she covers her mouth so she doesn't wake me.

"Mommy, are you sleeping?" she whispers really softly.

I can hear her moving closer. I wait for the perfect moment when I know her face is close. My eyes spring open and I grab her. She screams with laughter as I haul her into bed with me kissing her face all over.

"Got you!" I tickle her belly and she laughs harder trying to hold my hands so I quit tickling her.

I laugh, pulling her up for a cuddle and sticking her under the blanket with me. "Good morning, baby." I kiss her forehead, feeling overwhelmed once again with my love for her.

She smiles at me, showing her cute little missing teeth. She has a small smattering of freckles across her nose and beautiful green eyes with dark hair. "Good morning, Mommy. What's for breakfast?"

"Eggs and bacon sound good?"

She nods enthusiastically. "Go get dressed for school, I will be in the kitchen." She hops off the bed and runs to her room, how I wish I had an ounce of her energy.

I turn on the stove letting it get hot and turn on the sink to wash a glass sitting inside.

I see a girl in a pair of jeans and a t-shirt running straight for my house.

What the heck is going on?

I take out my phone calling Etta, putting it on speaker. "Good morning, sister." She yawns through the phone.

"Etta, there is some girl running through my backyard straight to my house right now. Should I be concerned?" I inquire, feeling kind of uneasy about the whole thing.

As she gets closer, I can finally see her face and it's Rosie. She is the girl that Etta rescued last night.

16

"It's Rosie!" I tell Etta.

She cusses over the phone and I can hear her running through the house. I open my door and Rosie runs up the steps collapsing at my feet, exhausted.

She literally ran probably two miles or so.

"What's the matter, honey?" I ask her. She is shaking hard in the morning air. I step inside the house and grab a throw blanket, wrapping it around her.

She looks at me, her mouth trembling. "I looked outside. I saw his vehicle outside of the gate and I ran. He can't find me." She clutches onto my pajama pants and I'm immediately concerned that she saw him outside of the gate.

I wrap the blanket tighter around her, helping her to her feet. I lead her into the house and lock the door. I can hear Etta shouting things through the phone. I set Rosie at the bar.

Michaela is getting drive-thru this morning, I tell myself as I turn off the stove.

She looks around my house and I take her in. She's so young; I am looking at a twelve-year-old little girl only five years older than my baby and she was forced into marriage.

Her world has been torn completely apart.

Michaela runs down the stairs and stops dead in her tracks when she sees Rosie. "Sweet girl, we will go to the drive-thru and get breakfast. This is Rosie. Rosie this is my daughter, Michaela."

Rosie waves at her through the blanket. "Mommy do you want me turn on the heat for her?"

My sweet angel baby, I walk over to her and hug her. "You are so thoughtful, yes honey." It saddens me but she is used to seeing women and kids in sad situations, she is so smart beyond her years.

She runs into the living room to turn on the heat. I walk to the cabinet and grab a banana for Michaela to tide her over, bringing it to her in the living room. "Do you want to watch TV until it's time for us to leave?"

She nods and turns on a cartoon as I see a vehicle pulling up my drive. "Etta is here, Rosie." I stop talking when I see she is not where I left her.

I run around the bar and I don't see her anywhere. What the heck? I run through the house trying to find her and the only place left is Michaela's room.

"Hi, Michaela. Where is your mommy?" I hear Etta say.

I stick my head over the railing. "I'm up here, Rosie is hiding somewhere," I tell her.

Etta runs up the stairs and we both go in Michaela's room, that's when I spot her foot sticking out the end of Michaela's bed.

I look at Etta, it saddens me she is so scared. "Hi sweetheart, you okay?" I get down onto my knees beside the bed.

"Who is here?" She sticks her head out of the bed just enough to see me and Etta, who is next to me.

She slowly slides out from under the bed. "It was just me, sweetheart. I am going to take you back to the compound."

She takes Etta's hand. "I saw him outside of the gate," she tells her and I look at Etta unsure what to say. It's highly unlikely that it was him but a similar vehicle.

"Did you see his vehicle?" I ask her.

She shakes her head no. "No, he was pressing the buttons on the gate trying to get in."

Wait what?

Etta's eyes widen at her words and my heart picks ups a little. "I need to get the cameras checked."

She takes out her phone and I watch over her shoulder as she scrolls back through the recordings until we see someone getting out of an older beaten down SUV. He is wearing black clothes like he is in mourning. He looks at the compound and starts fiddling with the alarm system.

Oh my God, she is right!

"I need to go check on Michaela." I run down the stairs and she is still on the couch watching TV.

I double check the locks before I walk back upstairs. "I need to go take Michaela to school and I will be back. Do you want me here or the compound?" I ask Etta.

"The compound. We're getting some of the guys to come over and escort us over." Etta helps Rosie off the ground and I wrap the blanket around her tighter.

The horror of what she is having to face, when she thinks she is safe for only to have him show up out of the blue.

I leave her in the care of Etta needing to take Michaela to school. It's hard for me to leave when someone needs me.

3

LYNN

ONE WEEK LATER

IT'S BEEN A LONG WEEK. Rosie has been the hardest we have had to adjust. The second she saw her husband outside of the compound, it set her back very far.

Fear is such a powerful thing, it can control everything, every aspect of your life until you learn to overcome it.

She has experienced fear her whole life and it's hard for her to not let it rule her life.

But today is my niece and nephew's birthday party; it's hard to believe they are five years old.

I get out of my SUV when Etta walks over so we can go in together. "Hey, sister," she greets me.

Michaela takes her moment to escape and run straight through the gate to play with the kids.

I bite back the overwhelming feeling I get when I see the amount of people inside of the backyard through the gate.

I seek out Michaela to make sure she is okay; she is going down the slide with Sariah, my niece.

Lani waves at us from the food table where she is setting everything up. "So Rosie is seeming to do a little a better." I stop talking when I notice Etta is focusing on a man across the yard next to Lane.

He smiles at her and she looks away so fast I am not sure she doesn't get whiplash. I peek over at Konrad. I have met him a few times and he is a really great guy.

I grin at Etta, she glares at me. "Stop that!" she hisses at me.

But that doesn't deter me. "Girl, I saw that look between the both of you! Konrad is a great guy," I encourage her. I want her to be happy and I want her to get out there, meet someone great for her.

Her eyes widen. "Wait, you know him?" she asks me, scooting closer to me.

I nod. "He volunteers with the boys. He takes them out for the day sometimes." I see the soft look on her face at that knowledge, knowing he is good with kids.

She is so selfless, she is always taking care of everyone and protecting all of these girls. I want someone to protect her and care for her as she does the others.

"Stoppp." Etta pushes my shoulder slightly, growing red at my knowing look. I giggle and cover my mouth at her reaction.

Vinny walks over breaking the moment. "How does it feel, the babies being five?" Etta asks Vinny.

We have watched our brother and his family grow over the years. It's been so beautiful to see the love they have for each other.

Vinny gives us a sad look. "It's fucking hard. One second they were small enough to hold them in one hand and now they're tearing down the house." He stares off into space, deep in thought.

Then he gets a secret grin on his face. I suck in my lips knowing what he is going to say the second he saddles up closer to Etta. "So, I saw that look." I burst out laughing, Etta blushes so hard that it makes me laugh harder.

She gives us the stink eye. "Shut up." She looks like she is ready to punch the both of us.

Vinny joins in with his laughing. "Etta, you almost knocked him on his ass. When you looked away, he had to grab onto the porch to keep standing."

She gets a sly smile on her face, her whole mood changing. "That does make me feel better."

I wrap my arms around her. "I love you, Etta."

She hugs me back. "I love you too." She walks inside the house leaving me with Vinny who is watching her leave.

"I do want her to find happiness, she deserves it."

Vinny studies me, he puts his hand on my shoulder. "But so do you Lynn, you deserve for someone to care for you the way you do for everyone."

He leaves me standing by myself, leaving me deep in my thoughts. Having a relationship is something that I haven't allowed myself to think about.

I notice that Lee, one of the weird uncles that is friends with Caleb, who is Vinny's son, goes into the house too. I start to follow but Konrad and Lane go in after him.

I look to the little boy who is Lee's nephew. I only know Lee's name because he introduced himself to me earlier this year. But the dad, I have no clue of his name. He never speaks to anyone and just watches his kid.

I turn around to check on Michaela to make sure she is okay before I dive back into my thoughts.

The first couple of years after leaving the cult, I was concentrating on my school and becoming a therapist.

The last few years though, in bed at night I think about maybe sharing that with someone, Michaela having a father figure in her life. She has amazing male figures without a doubt, but I want her to have that special bond with someone.

I want to spend my life with someone. I was forced into marriage at thirteen years old. I never had the chance at anything real, it was hell those three years.

But I see all of the guys with their women, how well they are treated and I get to see how in love they are.

I want that for myself, to just know that no matter what, I will have my person.

I am so lost in my thoughts that I barely notice Etta running out of Vinny's house with a slight paleness to her face.

"Are you okay?" I ask her when she gets closer to me. "I saw Lee run inside after you, along with the guys." I take her hand.

She shrugs her shoulders. "It was really weird. He wanted to speak to me, but I told him no, that I was uncomfortable. He was standing outside of the bathroom when I opened the door."

I look over my shoulder and spot Lee walking out of the gate; good thing he is leaving. I don't want him here, especially around Etta.

"What the fuck? I have noticed that he is creepy for a while now," I confess to her.

She cringes. "Wait you have noticed too? I thought I was paranoid."

I nod, looking over at the gate to make sure that he isn't slipping back in. "I have seen him staring at you and Michaela more than once."

That was not the right thing to say. Her face and mood change right before my very eyes. I can feel the rage coming off her in waves. "I should have shot him," she grinds out between clenched teeth.

I honestly never even noticed that he was weird until Michaela mentioned that he has been staring at her a lot. I have been on red alert ever since.

"Did Michaela notice?" Etta asks.

I look at the ground wishing I would have mentioned it to the guys. "She's the one who told me."

Etta turns around on her heel and runs out of the gate straight toward Lee.

What the fuck!

I look around for someone to go to her with me when I see Konrad and run to him. My heart is pounding in my chest at the prospect of her being hurt. "Etta just ran after Lee, I let it slip that he made Michaela uncomfortable."

Konrad takes off at a full sprint and I follow after him and I see some of the other guys following me. My eyes search the parking lot for her. I see her down the lot toward a car. Konrad is way ahead of me since he is faster.

Lee has his hand up in the air like he is going to punch her in the face. I put my hand over my mouth terrified out of my mind. I start to scream to warn her or something, but Konrad makes it to her, pulling her back out of the way before he could hit her.

He moves and stands in front of her, putting her out of harm's way. I make it over to her, feeling majorly sick to my stomach because I was so scared for her.

Konrad grabs his fist, laughing. "Big fucking mistake." He twists his fist and I can hear the sickening sound of bones breaking.

"Please let me go." He falls to his knees onto the ground.

"Please let me go," Konrad mocks him, twisting and tightening his hands. "I won't let you fucking go, you DARED to hit her!" he roars at him, Lee flinches.

Etta is pale; pale in a way I have never seen before and that terrifies me. She looks at me and then down at Lee. "I think he's from the cult," Etta whispers. "He said, 'it's not my place.'"

I freeze at those words, words we have heard for so long and so many times over our lifetime.

Etta is shaking hard. I take her hand holding onto her, to give her strength. Konrad takes out his phone and I know he is texting the others to come to us.

Lee starts screaming at the top of his lungs, "Get the fuck down!" Konrad yells at him, pushing his face into the gravel hard.

Konrad looks at Etta, who is not herself and far from it. "Etta, look at me. You are safe, no one can hurt you here."

She takes a deep breath and I join her, my mind is reeling at this. "Tell me who the fuck you work for," Etta demands, he struggles to get away. "Tell me or I will shoot off your dick. You have no other choice. Know your place, fucker." She throws his words right back at him.

"Tell me now!"

He looks at us all wide-eyed. "DANIELSON," he screams at her.

I take a step back like I have been burned in disbelief that he is actually from the cult.

Konrad tells the guys that he tried to hit Etta.

Everyone around us is looking slightly confused as to what is happening. "Danielson is the cult we grew up in."

I decide to make my presence known, moving closer to Lee. I am scared but I am grown now, my husband is dead. "Why are you here after so many years?" I ask, Vinny wraps his arm around me tightly.

"You took my fiancée." He looks directly at me when he says it and not at Etta.

I blink in confusion. Everyone is quiet as we think of who his fiancée could be but he continues to stare at me, anger growing on his face.

Then it hits me and it hits me hard as to what he is meaning. My heart stops, everything in me freezes with fear unlike I have ever felt before.

"No!" I scream at him.

He is here for Michaela.

Etta takes off running toward the party and I am right behind her. I need to get to my baby, I need to make sure she is okay and in my arms.

I can't even breathe, I am not sure how I even made it inside of the gate it's such a blur.

I start looking around the yard to see if I can see her, but I don't see her anywhere. My heart is beating so fast, it feels as though it is literally beating out of my chest.

"Where is Lani?" Trey screams and I realize I don't see her either.

Oh my God.

I turn toward the house following Etta. Everyone is looking through the house and I look out the window. Lani is holding onto Michaela who is getting dragged by the guy that came with Lee.

"NO!" I scream as they are getting further and further away.

Please dear God, hold on Lani! Don't let my baby go.

We all run out of the house. Michaela is screaming at the top of her lungs and that is a sound that will haunt me for the rest of my life.

I take off in the field toward them when I see a motorcycle pull in right behind them. He gets off the bike. "Tristan, help!" Etta screams at the man.

I move past everyone, the need to get to my baby is overwhelming.

Tristan's head whips in our direction and takes in the scene and runs to them since he is much closer; he makes it way before we do.

Tristan rips the guy off of Michaela and pushes him onto the ground, beating the shit out of him right in front of everyone.

I fall to the ground by my daughter, my legs not able to hold me up anymore once I reach her. I pick her up and put her in my lap, holding her so tightly.

My heart is hurting so bad, I'm physically sick with what just happened.

I rock her side to side. "Oh my God, my baby," I whisper, holding her even tighter, my baby completely staring off into space and frozen with fear.

Trey is holding Lani who is crying hard. She saved my baby, didn't allow her to be taken.

I try to ignore the man laying beside us, knocked out from Tristan, but I want to rip him to pieces for what he just did to my baby.

"Thank you for saving my niece." I hear Etta say.

I lean back, looking at Michaela to make sure she is okay but she is lifeless still, in shock with what happened.

"I am so thankful I was here, I just got back from my last mission."

I turn to look at the man that saved my daughter, my eyes filled with tears at the horror of what could have happened and what she would have been through. It's killing me knowing she is so scared.

"Thank you so much," I tell him, my voice cracking. I hold Michaela tighter against me rocking her like she is a small child.

"I need to get her home." I stand up, struggling to pick her up with me.

Tristan steps in front of me and I look into his piercing blue eyes. "I'll take you home. Can I carry her for you?"

At that Michaela snaps out of her shock, looking at me and then at Tristan before she nods, reaching her arms out to him. I am surprised that she went to him, but I guess him saving her has earned him her trust.

I hold my breath, waiting for what he is going to do.

He puts his hands under her arms and lifts her easily, she cuddles into his chest closing her eyes.

"Lynn, we will fix this shit," Trey tells me and a tear slides down my face at the reminder of what just happened.

My world just crashed around my feet.

It was my job, all that I wanted was to protect my baby. I wanted to give her the life that she deserves and I should have had.

Then this happened.

I feel like such a failure as a mother because I didn't protect her, I wasn't there for her.

I look at Lani, my heart so thankful for her and for what she has done. I walk to her wrapping my arms around her tightly. "Thank you so much."

She nods against me. "I am so glad that I was here."

I look at my brother Vinny who is pained, I can see it written all over his face but right now I need to be with my baby. I walk over to my car where Tristan is putting her in her seat like he has done it a hundred times.

Etta is standing next to me watching. "Wait, what happened to the little boy that was with them?" Etta asks.

"I will go look for him. Lane, can you watch him?" Konrad says, running toward the backyard we all just left.

"I'm going to take them home," Tristan tells Etta, taking my hand. I look down at his hand in mine, shocked that he did that.

He opens the door for me and helps me inside, putting my seat belt on me and gently shuts the door.

I look into the back seat at Michaela whose eyes are closed, exhaustion taking over.

Tristan gets in and starts my car and he looks over at me. "Are you okay?" he asks.

I look down at my hands. I am not okay, I am not sure if I ever will be. All of the horrible things that have happened to me in my life are nothing compared to the fear I just had over Michaela.

I would take every single pain from her if I could.

I shrug my shoulders. "That was the worst moment of my life, I thought I lost her," I confess.

He grips the stirring wheel hard; I can hear the leather cracking beneath his hands.

His eyes go to the mirror, I know he is checking on Michaela. I just want to go home, climb into bed with her and forget that this happened.

He said he was her fiancé.

Tristan

SHE IS COMPLETELY TORTURED by what happened, staring into space, pale and her hands are shaking.

It's fucking killing me, I don't even know what the fuck is happening, who that guy was taking the little girl.

Michaela's deep breathing in the back seat is the only sound in the SUV.

I have never met Lynn, the last six years I have been barely home and spent most of my time overseas. I have heard of her, seen her in passing, but never met her officially.

"What happened?" I need to know if they are in danger, if I need to be on my toes. Obviously Michaela is in danger because someone tried to take her right from a MC member's yard.

"I will explain later, I don't want kid ears hearing this," she tells me softly so not to wake Michaela.

I nod and the drive to her house is quick. No one fucking told me how beautiful she is, I'm pissed about that. She tells me the code to get inside her gate, her house is a white farmhouse with dark shutters.

"I will carry her in for you," I tell Lynn before she can get out.

She nods and I walk around the back of the SUV handing her her keys. I open the back door, unbuckling Michaela, picking her up gently. Lynn helps me with her so I don't jostle her awake.

I follow behind Lynn into her house and into Michaela's bedroom. I lay her down and Lynn tucks her into bed with her stuffed animal under her arm.

She motions for me to follow her, I do so and I can't help but think of how beautiful she is; her beautiful dark hair hanging loosely down her back, the pair of jeans and t-shirt highlighting the silhouette of her body.

"Want to join me?" She motions to the couch and I sit down next to her, putting my hands under my legs so I don't accidentally touch her, hold her hand like I fucking want to.

She pushes her long hair over her shoulder, grabbing a blanket off the back of the couch, covering her legs with it.

She looks at me with her large green eyes, just like her daughter. "I was raised in a cult. I am sure you knew this considering you have helped Etta in a few missions when you were home. I was forced into marriage a few days after I turned thirteen years old and Etta was fourteen when she was married. I had my sweet baby around a year after I was married."

Lynn

THIS IS ALWAYS SO scary to me, to tell others of my past because you never know the reaction you will get from people.

Plus, I don't want him to feel sorry for me.

I have come to terms with my past, but in the end, I got the greatest blessing in my life. I have healed, but some parts of me will never fully heal and I have accepted that fact.

I won't let it burden me.

His eyes grow dark, his expression to one of pure rage and it's scary. He is a big man, huge more like it, with tattoos starting at his neck trailing down to his hands. He reaches out like he wants to touch my hand but changes his mind at the last second, putting it beside us.

"Today, Lee said that he was Michaela's fiancé and that I stole him from her." Those words leaving my mouth are crushing, so deep, the raw pain hits me like a ton of rocks. Someone sat down and planned this. To marry off my baby.

That will never ever happen, but the thought that they went

to the extreme of enrolling a child in the same school as Caleb and Sariah just to get close to us, to her. Then tried to kidnap her.

He is a grown man, in his thirties, and he is looking at my baby as his fiancée. How can this be?

Who made those decisions? My husband is dead, my father is dead, my mother is alive. I look at Tristan as the thoughts hit me hard, she would have been the one to negotiate that deal. She is the only one left.

Tristan's angry face drops at my expression. "My mother must have done this, there is no one else left in the cult." It sickens me to even utter the words.

I was going to get my daughter out no matter the cost and I wouldn't have let anyone hurt her. I never knew how powerful a mother's love was until I had my daughter. Then the hurt set in that my mother didn't protect us, she let things happen that shouldn't have because she witnessed it with her very eyes.

No one protected us, but each other.

I pull the blanket further up to my chest cuddling it, needing the comfort. Tristan is staring at me, his eyes taking me in.

I look over at him, his face blurry as I fight back the tears that are dying to be shed.

"Darlin," his deep, southern voice drawls.

My lip trembles as fear strikes me once more. "Lee is still out there, he got away when we went to find Michaela. We all thought someone was going to stay with him, but everyone panicked to go find her. She's in danger."

That's when the height of anger really set in.

His whole body hardens, his jaw set. "She isn't in any danger, I'm here."

My heart skips a beat at his words. Oh boy.

4

LYNN

THREE HOURS LATER

MICHAELA IS STILL deep asleep so I'm in the kitchen making spaghetti, her favorite. Much to my surprise Tristan is still here and helping me with dinner.

I decided to let her sleep as much as she needs, her body and mind need the rest from the horrible shock of everything.

"So you're a therapist?" Tristan asks, bringing me out of my thoughts.

I look over at him while stirring the sauce and I nod. "I am, I specialize in trauma and PTSD."

He leans back against the counter, arms crossed studying me.

My hand trembles under his intense gaze. "What?" I ask, smiling slightly the longer he stares at me. He steps a little closer, putting the knife into the sink. I am hyperaware of everything that he is doing.

He is so attractive I would have to be blind to not notice it.

"You're kind of fucking amazing you know that?" he says out of the blue, totally rocking me.

My mouth drops open, shocked. "What?" I'm so confused to what would make him think that.

He grins at me slightly. "From what I have seen today, darlin, you had a baby at fourteen, raised her as a kid yourself. Escaped a fucking cult, became a therapist to help others like yourself and a damn good mom, with a great heart." His hand touches my forearm, sliding down my hand. "You're unreal."

I can't feel my legs, I am not sure if I even remember how to breathe. "Tristan," I whisper, speechless.

My heart hurts at his praise, something that I never expected but I never knew how much I needed to hear in the moment.

I can't resist the urge to be closer to him, I can feel the heat of his body when I move closer, looking up at him as I do so.

"Can I hug you?" I ask him.

He gives me the first blinding smile I have seen from him, it reaches his eyes completely, it's beautiful.

"Darlin, I would be hurt if you didn't."

Butterflies fill my stomach. He takes over, putting his hand on the back of my head and the other behind my back pressing me to his body. I am overwhelmed instantly, with the smell of his body, the warmth and most of all, the safety.

I have never felt as safe as I do in this very moment than I do with him, standing in my kitchen while the world is slowly crumbling around me.

But oh how I needed it. How I needed for someone to just take the burden for a minute and take comfort in someone else.

I just met him, just hours ago, so why does it feel like I have known him my whole life?

His fingers bury into my hair, I breathe in deep; it's silent in the kitchen besides the sound of the pasta boiling.

I tighten my arms around him, his body strong, hard. I can feel his calloused hands against my scalp from the hard labor.

He tilts my head back, so I am looking directly into his face and I lose my breath at the sight; the way he is looking at me, it's like he is just as affected.

A sharp piercing scream has me jumping back, gasping.

I turn around and run up the stairs to Michaela, my heart beating so fast, unsure of what to expect.

I push open her door and she is in the middle of her bed, holding her ears screaming.

"Baby, mommy is here!" I sit on the bed beside her, touching her face, wanting her to wake from the nightmare.

Tristan gets on his knees beside her and me. "Michaela, baby, it's okay. You're safe."

We both talk to her in soothing tones until she slowly pulls her hands from her ears and opens her eyes looking at the both of us.

That just killed me, wrecked me to my core. I never wanted for her to feel this kind of fear, experience nightmares. I never wanted this...

"Hi, Mommy." She smiles at me, her little toothless grin giving me a sliver of hope that she will be okay.

"Hi my baby girl, you feeling okay?" I ask her, rubbing her little hand.

She loses her smile. "I had a bad dream about the bad man trying to take me."

I want to kill him, I want to hurt him in ways that will never ever leave him and he will suffer for all of entirety. I am terrified that she won't be the same little girl from before this.

Right now, she is around Tristan, took comfort from him earlier and that gives me hope that she can get through this.

Tristan slowly reaches his hand for her to take. She looks at me to get my permission and I nod, smiling.

"Michaela, can you look at me?" he asks her gently. She gives him her full attention wearily. "I want you to know how sorry I am that happened to you, but I also want you to know that you will never ever see him again. I will make sure of that."

She looks at him full of hope. "Promise?" her little sweet voice asks him, his face shows his pain just as I am feeling.

"I promise, sweetheart. You're safe with me always."

She smiles again, her eyes a little lighter. "Okay," she trails off and I realize she doesn't even know his name.

"Tristan."

"Nice to meet you, Tristan," she states in a polite voice that's way too mature for her age and I giggle slightly at his amazed expression.

Then she gets a sly look on her face, looking at me and then to Tristan. "I guess that means you're moving in, sleepovers every night." She sits back in bed with her arms behind her head.

I laugh out loud at that, Tristan does too. "I am not sure if Tristan can stay with us honey, he may have plans." I give him a way out.

She looks horrified at the idea; he better plan then to spend time with her watching *Frozen*.

"Nah, I need to be with my special little lady and keep her safe." He winks at her and she is so gone- hook, line, and sinker.

I have to say, mommy can't blame her.

"Dinner is ready, spaghetti!" I give her a look at the word spaghetti.

She gasps dramatically. "Spaghetti?" she screams and runs straight down the stairs as fast as her little legs can carry her.

I laugh and follow right behind her. She is already in the kitchen holding a plate when I reach her.

"I will fix your plate baby, go sit at the table." I bend over and kiss the top of her head. "Wait, grab your drink first."

Tristan takes Michaela's plate from me. "Go sit with her, I will fix the food."

My mouth opens and closes. "I can get it." I start to take the plate back but he lifts it out of the way before I can do so.

He grins at me and my effort trying to take it back. "When is the last time someone waited on you?" he asks.

I try to think back to when and I honestly can't remember. Maybe when I was at home with my brother.

He notices my look and nods to the living room. "That's what I thought."

I start to say that he doesn't need to do this but his look is letting me know that this is not up for discussion. I walk into the dining room and sit beside Michaela who looks confused as to why my hands are empty.

Before I can explain, Tristan comes out holding two plates setting them in front of us. Her eyes widen at the sight. "Wow, mom we are princesses."

My poor heart, the satisfied look on Tristan's face lets me know that her words hit him. "You are for sure that, princess."

She grins at me happily at him calling her a princess. He leaves and comes back with wine, two glasses, and his plate sitting directly beside of me.

Michaela twists her spaghetti with her fork studying Tristan. "You do look like a king though, mom is queen and I am obviously a princess." She takes a bite of her food, nodding to herself.

Tristan chuckles at her, anyone that is around her can't help but fall in love with her. She is perfect.

"What does the princess like to do?" Tristan asks her.

She sets down her fork dramatically. "Well I do love to play softball, that is my favorite," she says in a really sophisticated voice.

"Well, I used to play baseball. Maybe we can play together sometime?" he asks her.

"Oh my God! After dinner please, Mommy?" She puts her little hands under her chin giving me the biggest puppy dog eyes.

I smooth my hand on the back of her head. "Of course my baby, we will all go play."

She starts shoveling in her food fast so she can go play. We all dig into our food listening to Michaela talk random facts about softball, school, and other things that make her happy.

I was so scared that my baby would be a shell of the person she once was. I know that it's not over and it will take a while for the trauma to leave her but for right now?

She is my baby and that's all that matters, seeing that smile gives me hope.

I'M on the steps watching Tristan throw the ball to Michaela. She has the biggest smile on her face eating up all of the attention that he is giving her.

"Mommy did you see that?" she asks.

I nod. "You did so good, baby," I praise her and she jumps up and down happily. You can't help but fall in love with my sweet girl when she's around. Call me biased, but I think she is the best.

"Can we play tag?" she asks.

Tristan sets down the ball and I get off the steps joining in. As I put my hair up in a bun, I say, "Sure. Where is base?"

She looks, sees her swing set and points at it. "You have to sit down in the swing to be safe."

"Who is the tagger?" She mumbles to herself looking between me and Tristan before she gets a wicked look on her face looking at Tristan. "You are it!" she screams, taking off running toward the swings.

He eyes me and I take off before he can catch me. I can hear him laughing, his feet hitting the grass behind me as he gives chase. I start laughing too, turning around to see where he is and I scream when he's literally a foot away.

Michaela laughs so hard at me that she snorts. Just as I reach the swings, an arm bands around my waist, his lips go to my ear. "Gotcha." He lifts me off of my feet, hugging me to his front.

I try not to think of how it feels to have him against me. He sets me down and I put my hands on my hips glaring at the both of them. "I guess that means I am a monster!" I growl at them both, putting my hands out like I have claws.

Michaela screams, running to Tristan. "Carry me my prince, save me from the monster."

He picks her up and she points to the playset. "Take me to the castle!" I start toward them and he takes off running with her.

I give chase, growling the whole time. He sets her onto the playset, crawling up beside her. He is way too big to even fit inside but he does anyway.

"Well, where did they go?" I pretend that I don't see them, searching all around the play set.

"Oh my gosh, she didn't see us," I hear her whisper to Tristan, giggling.

"What is that sound I hear?" I ask, moving in the direction of her giggle. I can hear her shuffling around.

Tristan winks at me holding a hiding Michaela in his arms. I move closer, Michaela takes a peek at me and puts Tristan's hand over her face thinking that's going to hide her.

"Where did she gooooo?" I say in a singsong voice. She giggles again and I move so I am standing right next to the playset looking inside.

"What is this? Is this a piggy?" I reach out and take ahold of her toe. She screams with laughter at me tickling her.

"Oh man she got me!" She slaps her leg dramatically before she turns her evil grin to me and Tristan. "I will give you a minute head start to hide." She points her little finger at the both of us then covers her eyes.

Tristan gently sets her on her feet and jumps out of the playset straight to me, taking my hand. We take off to find somewhere to hide.

"In here!" I point to a large bush, pushing him inside and I follow behind him sitting between his legs.

We watch as she climbs down from the playhouse and looks around the yard trying to see if she can spot us.

"She is so fucking precious, Lynn; you have done an amazing job with her," he whispers to me.

I smile at that. "She is my life."

He puts his hand on my arms. "You are hers too."

My heart sings at that. I just want my baby to be happy, safe. That's all I want. I am trying not to think of the way we are sitting right now, his legs on either side of me, with his arms hanging loosely.

I can feel his breath on the back of my neck and I can't resist the urge to look back at him. Our eyes connect, his face serious as he stares at me. My hand goes to his knee, to brace myself.

His hand slowly reaches forward, touching my cheek softly, gently. "You're so beautiful." The way he is looking at me right now and the way he spoke those words, I know that he means it.

I smile, my cheek growing hot at his praise. "You're so sweet, thank you."

He grins shaking his head like he is in disbelief and he leans forward resting his forehead against mine.

We don't speak, don't move, we just sit here together taking in this moment. I don't know that to think, I sure don't know how I am feeling.

I just know that I don't want him to leave.

"Found you!" she yells and pushes the bush back, smiling at us. I laugh, pushing myself to my feet. "You sure did, angel."

"I think it's time for a bath and to relax before bed," I point out to her.

"Okay, Mommy. Can I wear my princess pajamas?" She takes my hand.

"Yeah, want to pick them out or do you want me to?"

"I can!" She takes off running leaving me with Tristan.

I'm unsure what to do. "So uh, I do have some of Vinny's

clothes if you want to wear them, if you're staying, which is totally fine if you don't but if you do," I ramble.

"That's fine, darlin."

I let out a deep breath, internally beating myself up. I take him in the house showing him the guest room. "This is the room where they stay when they are here, just check the drawers. You can sleep here if you want."

"Thanks."

I practically run up the stairs to check on Michaela, who is already in the tub. I sit down onto the toilet next to her, she looks at me. "Want to play Barbies with me?" she asks.

I sit down beside the tub so I'm closer, making the Barbie walk across the edge of the tub. "Mommy, why did the mean man try to take me?"

I close my eyes for a few seconds, the pain overpowering me. I set the Barbie down. "Baby, people sometimes do things, horrible things and we never know why."

She looks at the Barbie I sat down for a few seconds. "I was so scared, I thought I would never see you again."

I want to throw up, I want to hurt someone. I want to do something to help me with the pain I am feeling right now and the pain she has suffered.

"I will never, ever leave you, baby. I promise you. I know what happened today was scary, but it will never happen again, no matter what," I reassure her.

She picks up her Barbie, pretending for her to swim in the water. "I love you my sweet girl." I rub my hand down her hair, leaning forward to kiss her forehead. "I am so sorry this happened to you, but mommy will always be here with you."

"I love you too." She smiles and it's all forgotten again. "I bet I can make her dive!" she says, lifting the doll up above her head letting her go into the water.

I laugh. "Looks like she is a professional."

She nods. "She is my Barbie." She smirks like that is the

answer for everything. I laugh, rubbing the tear off my cheek that managed to slip past. "You got that right."

I sit back watching her trying not to think of the negativity of things and the what-ifs. What matters is she is safe and here with me.

I walk into her room and grab her pajamas for her to change into. "Stay inside of your room while I shower, okay?" I tell her.

I quickly jump into her shower, leaving the bathroom door open. This way I can peek out of the shower to check on her. I know this is probably overkill but I need this right now, I need to make sure she is okay and with me. The panic I felt today? It's something that will never leave me.

I let the tears fall, the water washing them away from my face as I let myself feel everything and let the pain out.

I rest my forehead against the wall, breathing deep. "Mommy, can we have popcorn and a movie when you're out?"

I clear my throat so it doesn't sound like I am crying to her. "Yeah, I will be out in a minute."

I can hear her TV turn on. I finish showering and I look down at the counter. I forgot to grab myself some clothes.

I wrap the towel around me tightly. "I will be back, I am going to get dressed."

She doesn't even acknowledge me, too busy watching SpongeBob. I open her door, turning around the corner hurrying toward my room when I hear footsteps coming up the stairs right by my room.

Oh my God.

I pick up speed hoping that he doesn't see me.

His head pops up over the railing, his eyes going directly to me in my little bitty towel that is covered in princesses, way too short and barely covering my bits.

I wait for him to turn his head to look away from me, but he doesn't.

He just moves closer, standing at the top of the stairs.

His eyes slowly move from the tip of my toes to my face, my body burning from his gaze.

I grip my towel tighter. "I need to get to my room," I stutter, moving to slip past him. He doesn't move away to give me room to pass. No, he stands there, my arm and side have to brush past him to get in my room. I hear him breathe in deep the second I am near him.

I slip into my room, shutting the door behind me, leaning against the door. I smile to myself. I feel an ache between my legs, a feeling that no man has ever given me, until now. I am in trouble.

5

LYNN

I SIT DOWN on the couch with Michaela beside me, Tristan on the other side of her. She's holding her Princess blanket tucked under her chin with her head in my lap and her feet on Tristan.

He looks at me, then her little feet and scratches the bottom of her feet tickling her. She laughs, moving her feet away from him. "Tristan, that is not nice." She gives him a fake glare.

"Well, what about this?" I ask her, lifting her arm so I can tickle her.

Her face turns red with her silent laughter, then Tristan joins in on her feet. "UNCLE!" she screams, scooting onto the floor to get away from us.

She pushes her hair out of her face. "You guys are no fair." She crosses her arms across her chest looking at the both of us before she gives Tristan a sly grin. Moving to him she whispers in his ear.

Both of them turn to look at me, I know I am in trouble.

"Wait a minute." I put my finger up trying to deter them.

"Where do you think you're going?" Tristan asks when I try to scoot away.

He grabs my feet stopping me, pulling me until I am lying flat on my back then the both of them attack me.

Tristan has my feet tickling me, Michaela tickling me everywhere, my face, arms, stomach.

Tears rolls down my face as I try to fight them both off, but not too hard because the sound of Michaela's laughter is enough to let them torture me forever.

"Have you had enough, hmm?" Michaela says right in front of my face, leaving her nose to nose with me.

I sit up, my eyes in slivers looking at Tristan. "I think we need to give him a taste of his own medicine."

She doesn't waste a second jumping on him like a monkey, I join her tickling his sides.

"Alright, you guys are in trouble!" He stands with us both under his arms, holding both of us in the air.

"Hey!" Michaela pokes his side, jolting him causing him to almost drop the two of us. He gently, but pretends to be rough, slams us onto the couch next each other. "Now who is the boss?" He tickles us both at the same time.

His eyes are showing his happiness. I want to reach out and touch his face, to touch those little lines by his eyes, his dimples on his cheeks.

He stops tickling us both, staring at me.

I wish I knew what he was thinking.

"Can we watch *Halloween Town?*" Michaela breaks the moment.

"Sure thing, sweetheart." I sit up, pulling my shirt back down from where he was tickling me.

I can feel his eyes on me; I am so hyperaware of him. My body feels so alive right now. What is happening to me?

Why do I like him like this? In five years, I have never given another man a second glance until today.

Until Tristan.

Tristan

FUCK, the way she was looking up at me? My heart almost stopped in my chest. Her beautiful eyes, it's like she was staring right into my fucking soul.

I saw her in that fucking towel and I almost swallowed my tongue. She is the most beautiful woman I have ever seen. It's not just her looks, but her heart and the way she cares for her daughter. I am fucking hooked.

But most of all? I am gone for that special little girl.

I never dreamed when I came home this very morning that I would be here, cuddled up on the couch next to them both eating popcorn, watching a movie.

I just can't fathom doing anything else.

This is where I belong.

I have never been more certain of anything in my life until now. I know that both of them are meant to be mine.

But first things fucking first. I have to find the fucker that dared to take Michaela along with finding the others who are responsible for those scars on Lynn's back I saw when she was in the towel.

One thing at a time, Tristan. One thing at a time. I thought that switching back to civilian life would be much harder, that I would struggle, but they have given me a purpose and I think that is what I needed.

An hour later, both of them are fast asleep next to me. I reach out touching Lynn's hand to wake her. Her eyes slowly open, looking straight at me, a small smile on her lips. Fuck! That's it for me. I am fucked.

"Want me to put her to bed?" I ask her.

She sits up, her hair sticking up on one side from where she was laying. I try not to laugh at how adorable she looks. "Thank you."

I stand up, reaching under Michaela and lifting her up

bringing her blanket with her. Lynn pushes open her bedroom door and I set her gently into her bed and tuck her in.

I just don't understand how someone could have hurt her, she's literally an angel. Lynn scoots in front of me sitting at the edge of the bed, staring down at Michaela. She smooths her hair back out of her face, kissing her forehead gently.

She reluctantly stands up leaving; I take her hand and lead her out of the room. I know she is fighting herself and doesn't want to leave. She leaves the door cracked so we can hear her and peeks her head back inside of her bedroom to make sure she doesn't stir.

She rubs her face; I can see she is so exhausted. "Lynn, you need to get some sleep," I whisper to her and gently take her hand, leading her to her bedroom.

I pull back her blanket. "Are you putting me to bed?" she jokes, but lets me help her into bed.

I pull up the blanket, tucking it under her chin. She stares up at me, the cutest smile on her face. I chuckle slightly. "I think sometimes you forget to care for yourself." I push a strand of her hair out of her face.

She gives me the softest, kindest look. I know she is affected by my words but I am affected by all of her and that little girl.

"Goodnight, Lynn." I walk out of the room turning off the light behind me. I don't want to leave her, I want to fucking crawl into that bed with her. I could sleep for years.

I peek in on Michaela one last time before I go downstairs to the guest room where I am sleeping for the night.

Lynn

Two Hours Later

I AM WOKEN to the sound of a bloodcurdling scream. I throw my blankets back and I don't even breathe as I make it to Michaela's room in a second.

I throw open her door, her bed is empty. My heart is frantic in my chest. The sound of Tristan's footsteps coming up the stairs matches the beat of my heart.

I can't find her.

I look under the bed, don't see her.

Tristan tears into the room, looking around to see what is happening but Michaela is still screaming.

I run into her bathroom. I see the top of her head between the toilet and the bathtub, she is holding her head between her hands.

I fall to my knees beside her. "Baby," I call to her wanting her to hear me.

She doesn't answer me.

I touch her forearms; she flinches in my hands before she turns to look at me. "Sweetheart," I call to her once more.

She drops her hands. "Mommy?" she asks like it's a question.

My throat is thick from me trying not to cry. "Yes baby, it's me." I resist the urge to pick her up.

She looks behind me to Tristan, then back to me. "I had a really bad dream."

My tears fill my eyes, threatening to spill over. "I know baby, I am here, nothing can hurt you."

She crawls out of the hole into my arms, wrapping her arms and legs around me tightly. "I was scared."

I put my hand on the back of her head, holding her to me. "I know baby, it's okay to be scared."

I look at Tristan, I can see the fire burning in his eyes from what has happened. I feel the same anger in my heart.

I want to make all of them suffer for what they have done to her. She is a baby and they brought fear into her life, something she should have never had gone through.

I feel like it's my fault, I left her alone when I should have been watching her. I move to stand with her in my arms, but she is too heavy.

Tristan puts his hands under my arms and lifts both of us up like nothing. I carry Michaela with me to my bedroom, I'm going to let her sleep with me.

Tristan follows behind me, helping us into bed. I put her beside me as best as I can.

I run my fingers down her hair, the back of her head to soothe her. "I will make her a therapy appointment tomorrow with one of my friends," I speak into the dim room to Tristan who is hovering.

He puts his hand on my back, I swear it's like he is trying to give me strength. Right now? I need all I can give to get through this with her.

I will do whatever it takes to make sure she is okay from this.

"That's a good idea, doll."

I close my eyes at the endearment, my body growing heavy as the exhaustion sets in.

Tristan

THEY FALL BACK ASLEEP in minutes but I can't leave them again. I walk into my room, grab my blankets and pillow and make a bed right beside them.

I close my eyes, my mind not relaxing as I strain for any kind of sound from Michaela.

An hour later I manage to drift off to sleep.

A COUPLE OF HOURS LATER, we are woken again by her blood-curdling scream that shakes me to my very fucking core.

I jump up off the floor to the other side of the bed so I can be closer to Michaela. Lynn is breathing hard, I know Michaela's scream scared her. Michaela looks around the room frantically like her kidnappers are going to be right in the room with her.

Michaela sees me and rushes into my arms, planting her face in my chest. I wince hoping that it didn't hurt her.

Lynn has her hand over her mouth, I know she is fighting with her emotions.

Fuck me, so am I.

"I'm going to sleep now," Michaela's voice is muffled against my chest, snuggling in deep.

I look at Lynn to makes sure she is okay with this. "Is this okay?" I ask her.

She nods and helps me get comfortable in bed. I lay on my back with Michaela lying in the crook of my arm and Lynn lying beside her, her hand on Michaela's side.

I want to pull her into me too, Lynn is so close I can feel her heat against the outside of my arm.

I lean my head back, closing my eyes. I know sleep won't happen for me but I hope they rest.

Lynn
The Next Morning

I WAKE up and instantly turn over to look at Michaela who has pretty much crawled on top of Tristan cuddling into his chest.

She slept most of the night, as long as he was holding her. I think he made her feel safe because he is the one that rescued her.

I look at the clock on the bedside table, it's eight o'clock in the morning. I need to text my friend to set up an appointment for Michaela. I know therapy will be a huge help to push her in the right direction. I lean over and take my phone off the nightstand shooting a quick text.

I know Etta has already canceled all of my appointments for the next week so I can concentrate on Michaela.

I feel eyes on me and I look over to see Tristan awake and damn, I don't want to admit how great he looks when he first wakes up.

Michaela stirs in his arms, her eyes slowly opening and moving around until she sees me. "Good morning, baby." I take ahold of her tiny hand.

She smiles sweetly at me. "Morning, Momma, Tristan," she says in her formal voice.

After a long, horrible night I needed to see that bringing a little light in the darkness.

"So, what do you feel like eating for breakfast?" I ask her.

She puts her little finger to her chin. "I think bacon, French toast, and some eggs are in order."

I laugh at her goofiness. Tristan sits up with her but she doesn't move to get away from him.

"How about you guys pile up in front of the TV and watch a movie while I cook breakfast?" I ask.

She grins happily. "Ohhhhh, I will go get my Barbies and we can play together, Tristan." She takes off from the bed in a sprint to her bedroom, leaving us alone.

He is watching me. "I want to thank you for everything you have done."

He reaches over and takes my hand that is buried in the comforter, my breath catches when his thumb rubs the top of my hand. "No need to thank me, honey. I want to be here."

His eyes look straight into my soul, I search his face for an ounce of hesitation. "You do?" I can't help but ask, I am vulnerable right now.

He scoots closer. "I wouldn't want to be anywhere else but here, with you two." I can hear the sincerity in his voice.

I smile, his words making me happy. He looks at me so softly, his hand touches my cheek, before his lips touch the top of my head in a tender kiss.

I decide to be open and honest, because I do like him. "I want you here too."

He shakes his head like he's in disbelief. He picks me up and pulls me against him in a tight hug and it's filled with so much warmth, protection, and safety that I could stay here forever.

"Did I tell you how beautiful you are in the morning?"

I sit back, my face burning from his compliment because I know I look rough. I touch the top of my head and I feel my hair literally sticking straight up. I slide off the bed running into the bathroom to fix that and I can hear his laughter behind me.

I look at myself in the mirror. Despite everything, I am happy.

LYNN

I HAVE STARED at the doors to the clinic where Michaela has been inside for an hour. I want to march inside and wrench her out of there, into my arms.

As a therapist, I know therapy is never easy. It's probably one of the most difficult and necessary things you will go through but it's even harder because she is my baby. I don't want her to hurt at all, I want to take it all away. She is inside away from me and I don't know if she needs me or not. I know Summer will take care of her, but it doesn't make it easier.

Etta and Konrad came to visit us earlier; I had a little breakdown with Etta. I really needed that cry and a release from it all.

There's a knock on the window. I jump looking out to see Tristan standing there with two drinks in his hands, a McDonalds bag, and another bag under his arm.

I unlock the door and he gets in the driver's side of my SUV. "For the doll." He hands me a Coke, then from inside the bag a burger and a large fries. I spot a Happy Meal inside of the bag, too. "A Happy Meal for the little lady." He puts it on her car seat.

My heart does that stupid little happy dance because he

thought of my baby. "Thank you, Tristan. You didn't have to do this," I tell him.

He gives me a look, a look that says I shouldn't thank him for that but I want to, it means a lot.

"Since the little lady is going to be inside of the clinic for another hour, I figured we could have our first date." I grin at his cuteness; he reaches into the other bag that he had. I see it's an iPad and a stand. "Dinner and a movie?" He winks.

I watch as he sets everything up, opening my food for me and turns on the fucking *Notebook*. Send help, because I am in trouble.

I don't say anything, I'm shocked because he put so much thought into this. "I know this is a lame first date."

I shake my head no, furiously. "No, this is amazing. I'm shocked you've done all of this," I admit.

I hate to admit it but when he smiles his eyes show who he truly is. He smiles happily, he 's so beautiful when he does that. When he's not smiling, he's a terrifying guy.

He is the guy who laid with and held my baby all night long so she didn't have nightmares, who tucked me into bed last night. I'm in trouble.

"So how long have you been single?" Tristan asks.

"Since I was sixteen, when I left the cult." He stops eating to look at me. "Really, no one has asked you out?"

I shrug my shoulder. "They have, I just wasn't ready mentally."

He studies me for a minute. "And now?"

I smile. "More than ready." I reach over and squeeze his hand, because I am. I am ready to have room in my life for someone.

"And you?" I ask, taking a bite of my fry. "Are you ready?"

"Without a single doubt."

My stomach clenches at the amount of butterflies I feel at his words, his eyes looking directly at me, so deep.

I smile. "What if she has a daughter?" My voice slightly trembles, my nerves getting to me a little.

He puts his hand on my face, so he can get my full attention. "Without a single doubt," he repeats his words.

"Okay then," I whisper, emotional.

He smiles, his thumb running across my cheekbone. "Okay then."

We turn back to the movie but I can't even focus on it because my mind is going a hundred different directions with what just happened.

The doors to the clinic open, Summer and Michaela step out. I hurry out of the SUV to my daughter with Tristan right beside me. "Can you put her in while I speak to Summer?" I ask Tristan.

He takes her hand, she skips to the vehicle. He hands her a kid meal and she screams with happiness.

"How is she?" I ask.

"Honestly, she's dealing quite well considering what has happened. Her nightmares are what are causing her the most distress right now, but if she is not improving within the next few weeks, maybe we can discuss medication for PTSD. Normally I wouldn't recommend having a man around after the trauma she has had, but their bond is amazing. He makes her feel safe and he is helping the process."

I let out a sigh of relief from hearing about how Tristan is helping her process and not hindering it. "They do have a great bond." I look over at them, Tristan is talking to her in the back seat.

Summer smiles at them both too. "Those MC men are different than most men, huh?"

Dying to get back to my daughter to see how she is doing, I ask Summer, "When do you want her back?"

"Tomorrow, I want to stay on top of everything with her."

"I will be back tomorrow." I start to turn around but she puts her hand on my arm. "You have a strong little girl, she will get through this without a doubt. Kids are so resilient." She is speaking as a friend and not my daughter's therapist.

"Thank you, I needed to hear that."

She smiles and walks back inside. I get into the SUV with Kids Bop blasting over the speakers. I look back at her, she is singing with a mouthful of fries in her mouth. I laugh. "Chew your food before you choke."

She hurries to chew her food so she can blast it through the car. "Where to now?" I ask.

"PARK!" she begs.

"To the park we go." Tristan puts the vehicle into drive.

The park is close to our house, we stop on the way at a gas station for drinks. The second we let Michaela out she sprints across the grass to the huge playground.

"She seems to be doing okay."

I nod in agreement, she is, she is doing really amazing considering. "The therapist said that her dreams are what are causing her distress, she goes back tomorrow."

Tristan gets a far-off look in his eyes. "Nightmares are really hard."

"I know what those feel like, I just wish she never had to experience those." My heart is breaking that she has to relive it.

"I will find the people responsible and I will kill them." I startle at the viciousness in his voice.

I know without a doubt that he means it with his whole heart. "Make me a promise?"

"What's that?"

I look at the playground where she is going across the monkey bars. "I call first dibs."

He grins sinisterly. "You got it."

I want to hurt them, I want to make them pay for everything they've done to me, to my baby and all of the people they have hurt their whole lives.

I won't stop until the fucking cults are destroyed.

First step is the person who claims to be my daughter's fiancé, he is going to be a lesson to all.

Mess with my baby, death is something you will be begging for. That is without a doubt.

"Mommy, can you swing with me?" she asks, breaking me from my evil thoughts. "I will be right there!" I yell back and make my way to her on the swings. "Tristan, can you push us please kind sir?" she asks.

"Why I sure can, little lady." He pulls her back, letting her go. She screams with laughter, throwing her head back enjoying the moment.

"Your turn, doll." He pushes me and her both at the same time. I smile at him. "Mom, I am going to beat you!" She kicks her little legs trying to go further than me.

"Are you sure you want to try to sleep in your room?" I ask her for the fifth time.

I tried to take her into my room, but she stopped me before I could. "Mommy, I don't think I will have nightmares tonight." She tries to sound brave.

"If you get scared, you can come get me anytime, okay?" I tell her, helping her into bed.

"Okay, Mommy."

Tristan walks over to the other bookshelf. "How about a princess story?" He takes *Beauty and the Beast* off the shelf.

I sit at the foot of her bed while he sits on the floor next to her; he starts to read to her, making sure she can see the pictures.

I watch the both of them together, his full attention on her. My heart is so full right now, watching them both.

A few minutes later her eyes slowly drift closed, her blanket tucked under her chin.

I slowly slide off the edge of the bed so I don't wake her. I turn on her sound box to have some white noise in the room and I turn on the baby monitor that I used to have when she was tiny, just in case.

Tristan puts the book back and turns on the bathroom light to give her a little light so it's not completely dark in the room.

I tiptoe out of the room, he follows behind me pulling her door halfway closed. "Do you want to watch a movie?" he asks me, taking me in.

I'm currently dressed in a really baggy shirt and shorts, my hair in a bun at the top of my head but the way he is looking at me, it makes me feel pretty.

"I would like that. Do you want to watch in my bedroom or downstairs?" I ask then internally wince, I don't want him getting the wrong idea or anything like that.

"Your bedroom is good. Want me to get you a glass of wine?" he offers.

I nod. "That would be great, I had some beer delivered for you today."

He smiles, happy that I thought of him. How can I not think of him? I think about him too much honestly.

He walks downstairs and I sprint to my bedroom, making my bed so it doesn't look frumpy. And now here I am standing here waiting for him to come up the stairs.

The second he sounds close to my bedroom, I slowly pull down the comforter so it just looks like I am just now unmaking it.

I slide into bed and pull the blanket over my legs, slightly chilled. He hands me my wine and I hand him the remote to find whatever he wants to watch.

"We didn't finish *The Notebook*," he points out and he turns on the movie, fast forwarding it to get to the part we were at.

I turn on the baby monitor so I can hear Michaela if she wakes up scared, then turn down the lights from the app connected to the lights.

I can feel him looking at me, I know I am fidgeting because I am seriously nervous. I have never invited a guy into my bed before like this. I finally gather my courage and look over at him.

He reaches over to me, I hold my breath waiting for his first touch. His finger glides gently across my cheekbone, pushing a stray hair off my cheek and behind my ear.

"You're beautiful," he says softly, his eyes hooded looking at me.

I blush, looking down at my lap to get away from the intensity of his gaze. "Thank you."

He puts his finger under my chin, lifting my head so I am looking at him again and not hiding. "You are welcome, I like your rosy cheeks."

He leans over to me and I grip my wine glass hard so I don't spill it everywhere. He licks his lips slowly, my insides shaking so hard the closer he gets to me. His eyes are on my lips, is he really going to kiss me? I want to scream and run out of the room because he is moving so slow, the intensity of it all killing me.

At the last second, I can feel his breath on my lips as his lips touch my cheek softly. "Tristan," I whisper, my hands going to his shoulders.

I feel him smile against my cheek, he lifts his face and he moves to the other cheek giving it the same amount of attention as the other.

I think he is trying to kill me.

I hold still, completely still.

He lifts his head once more, his eyes looking into mine. The sound of the movie playing in the background is completely forgotten because I think I could get lost in his eyes forever.

His hand glides up my neck slowly, cupping my face. "Tell me I shouldn't kiss you." His voice is rough, like he is fighting himself.

I decide to be brave; I deserve a real first kiss. "Why would I tell you that?"

He grins like I just gave him a million dollars, before he presses his lips against mine oh so softly, testing the waters.

I open my mouth to deepen the kiss, that's all he needs to take over and he does with the urgency of a dying man.

He kisses me in a way that has every hair on my body standing on end, goosebumps breaking out across every inch of my skin and I feel it from the tips of my toes to the top of my head.

This is everything.

Emotions wreck me. I try to fight back the tears because this is what I have missed my whole life. He pulls back and I look at him. I know he sees the tears in my eyes because his face is horrified.

"Baby, did I make you cry?" He catches one of my tears as it falls down my face.

I shake my head no. "It's not you, that was just my first real kiss is all," I admit, it doesn't do me any kind of justice to keep things inside.

I can see the fire in his eyes at the realization of my words. I fight back the shame that comes with the telling of others. But I will never allow myself to be ashamed for long, I am a survivor and I do not deserve to be anything else but that.

He pulls me to him, kissing my forehead gently before resting his forehead against mine. "Darlin, it fucking hurts me to my core that you have suffered any kind of pain in your life. You're so kind, sweet, and beautiful. How someone could touch an angel in any sort of way but with respect I will never fucking fathom." He sits back, angry. "The Sinner in me will make sure they die."

Oh fuck.

I know that he speaks the truth.

"It's all over, that part of my life is long gone," I reassure him.

He touches my hand gently, bringing it to his mouth kissing the back of it. "It's not over until they are all six feet under, until every member of that fucking cult is dead."

I don't say anything, I can't say anything, emotions have my throat clogged. I put my wine onto the nightstand next to me, turn off the light and practically face-plant into his chest.

The second my face touches him, I am in heaven. His arms wrap around me tightly, holding me like someone could wrench me away from him any second.

We watch the movie, or we pretend to. I am deep in my thoughts with everything happening around me.

It doesn't take long for me to fall into a deep sleep, I have never felt safer in my life. It's intoxicating.

I WAKE up to the sounds of Michaela talking. I look around the pitch-black room and see the light of the baby monitor is on.

I lean over turning up the volume. "Shh, it's just a dream, baby." I hear Tristan soothe her.

I rush out of bed, hating that I didn't hear her and I make it to her room in seconds.

Tristan is lying in bed beside her, running his fingers over her forehead into her hair.

She is already back asleep; he reaches out with his free hand for me. I walk over taking his hand, he pulls me to him. We sit and wait until she is back into a deep sleep before we sneak back out of the room.

"I am a horrible mother, I didn't hear her wake up." I beat myself up, rubbing my face hard.

I know I am being irrational right now, but I am so emotionally exhausted. He pries my hands away from my face gently. "You are not a bad mother, you are far from it. I heard her talking in her sleep, I knew it was a nightmare so I woke her. I wasn't asleep yet, doll," he reassures me.

He sets me down onto the bed, climbing in beside me and holding me close. "Thank you, for everything," I whisper to him in the dark, the only light coming from the room is the baby monitor.

He kisses my cheek. "You don't have to thank me for something I want to do." His hand slowly slides under my shirt and rests on my belly.

I cringe at that, because I have pudge that never went away after having Michaela. He runs his fingers across my skin and I burst out laughing because I am super ticklish.

He snorts and that brings out another bout of laughter from me, because I never expected to hear that sound from him.

"Alright, we need to get some sleep," he chuckles, pulling the blanket over me and pulling me a little closer.

I close my eyes; I fall asleep with a huge smile on my face.

7

TRISTAN

I WAKE up to the sound of little feet moving across the hardwood floor. My eyes pop open and I see little Michaela with her hair all mussed up and holding her blanket.

She looks at me then to her mother. I put my finger to my mouth and ease myself out of bed so I don't wake up Lynn.

She is so exhausted; I want her to sleep in if she can.

Michaela lifts her arms like she wants me to pick her up, my fucking heart warms that she wants me to hold her. I pick her up and she rests her head against my shoulder, I have always felt the urge to protect everyone around me.

But with her and Lynn? It's raw, it's intense, I would do anything and everything to make sure they are protected. I would destroy the whole fucking world for them and I wouldn't hesitate.

"Do you want me to make you some breakfast?" I ask. She nods, yawning.

I take that as my answer carrying her down the stairs. I turn the TV onto a cartoon, covering her with her little blanket on the couch. She smiles at me and I could float out of the fucking room at that.

Lynn

I JOLT AWAKE. I look at the clock and I see it's nine o'clock. I haven't slept in this late in a long time. I feel the mattress where he was sleeping, it's cold so he must have been up for a bit.

I can smell bacon floating through the bedroom, Tristan must be making breakfast.

I have taken Michaela out of school for the rest of the week to get her readjusted after what happened.

I make my way down the stairs and I spot Michaela vegging on the couch, watching TV.

She looks up at me when she hears the stairs creak. "Good morning, my baby." I lean over the back of the couch kissing her cheek.

"Morning." Her little voice is so sweet in the mornings.

I walk into the kitchen, excited to see Tristan who is slaving away at the stove flipping bacon. "Good morning."

He looks over at me, his eyes lighting up. I walk over to him. "What do you want me to do?" I ask.

He wraps his arm around my back, pulling me to him, kissing my lips sweetly. My eyes flutter closed at the feel of him.

He kisses my cheek before he lets me go. "You can help me by cuddling on the couch with your baby."

My stupid stomach does the flipping thing again. "Okay." I lean forward and hug him.

Just as the bacon pops loudly, I'm hit in the arm with grease. "OUCH!" I jerk away from the stove.

I can see the panic in Tristan's eyes as he drags me to the sink to rinse off my arm. "It barely got me, I'm okay," I tell him. His hands are shaking. "Hey, I'm fine. See." I point to the barely there mark.

He lets out a deep breath. "Fuck I can beat up the fucking bacon for hurting you," he grumbles.

I snort laugh so hard, dropping my forehead against his chest. "You're adorable." I hug him tightly, wiping the tears from my eyes from the laughter.

He rolls his eyes at me, but I can tell he is happy. "Now go spend time with Michaela. I saw they opened a new trampoline place in town. Maybe we can take her after her appointment?" he suggests.

My heart warms that he is thinking of my baby. "She would absolutely love that, she has mentioned that she wanted to go." I hug him once more, walking into the living room.

I sit next to her and she immediately lays her head against me. "How did you sleep last night?" I ask her, smoothing her hair out of her face.

"I had a few dreams but they weren't too scary." She tucks her blanket tighter under her chin.

She has had this same blanket since she was a baby, she has to sleep with it every night. When she was small, I would have to sneak and wash it while she was napping.

"I'm glad you slept better last night, baby." She nods her little head. I know she is still tired.

I think a nap is in order for her after breakfast so she can rest up for her appointment later.

It's hard for me to see my baby in therapy like this. Therapy is so helpful but healing is not easy, it's painful and sometimes you think you will never get better.

But you do.

You learn to deal with it the best way you know how, that is what's important. I would take away that fear from her in a heartbeat.

What's going on inside of her mind wondering why someone would do that, why they would hurt Lani, trying to get her to let her go, just so they can take her.

My poor angel.

My nose burns from the unshed tears. I just want to wrap her up and hold her tight and protect her from the world.

I am in awe of her though, she is doing so great considering everything that has happened. She is my strong little baby.

"I love you more than anything, my sweet girl." I kiss the top of her head, emotional.

She cranes her neck back to look at me, showing me her little toothless grin. "I love you too, Mommy."

I pick her up, straining as I do so since she is getting so big, hugging her tight. She hugs me back, letting me have this moment.

Tristan comes around the corner with a spatula in his hand. He takes in the scene and he mouths to me, "Is she okay?"

I nod, smiling.

"Breakfast is ready," he says softly so he doesn't startle her.

She jumps out of my lap in a split second charging her way to the kitchen, the cuddles long gone. I follow behind her. Tristan is already filling up her plate for her and hands it off so she can carry it to the dining room.

Then he hands me a plate filled to the brim with food, it's enough to feed three people. "This is your plate, right?" I ask, trying to hand it to him.

"Oh no, it's for you. You need to eat more." He backs away from me filling his own plate with a whole lot more than he gave me.

"You want me to get fat, huh?" I tease him on the way to the dining room. He sits down beside me with Michaela in front of us.

He shrugs. "I wouldn't care if you were six hundred pounds and bedbound."

I let my head drop to the table. "You're absolutely nuts." I crack up picturing him just bringing me loads and loads of food.

He laughs with me, Michaela joins in too and I know she has

no idea what we are talking about but it's funny to her none-theless.

"It is a good show though."

My head shoots up and I look at him incredibly. "Wait, you watch *600-Lb. Life?*"

He chuckles. "Honey, I have spent so much time overseas, I have watched every show known to man when I had downtime."

"Well, we will have to watch that later and *90 Day Fiancé.*"

He points his bacon at me. "Darlin, if you think that is going to cause me distress, you are sorely mistaken."

"Well, it's date night for us tonight."

He winks. "Anything to spend more time with you."

Michaela is looking at the both of us confused, her brow furrowed. "Are you guys flirting?"

I almost choke on my food; I cough loudly trying to catch my breath. I look at Tristan in panic.

"We were," he just admits to her like it's nothing.

"Oh okay," she says simply and goes back to her food like she didn't just rock my world.

Tristan is shaking with silent laughter as he watches me. I know my face is so red right now because I can feel the heat from my skin burning me.

"It's not funny," I grumble, giving him the stink eye and he just laughs harder.

Loser.

Lynn

THE WAIT for her to come out of the appointment was even worse than yesterday I think, the hours go by so slowly.

Tristan decided that we needed another movie date. He had

a cute little movie picked out and had burgers delivered to us by one of the prospects.

I love how thoughtful he is.

Halfway through the movie he reaches over and takes my hand, holding it, our fingers intertwined. I can't resist the urge to lean over resting my head on his shoulder, my eyes on the iPad screen in front of us.

God, the way he feels, the way he smells.

I just can't deal.

The absolute crazy thing to me is that I am so comfortable around him, I never thought I would be.

Don't get me wrong. When I see men, I don't take off running terrified or anything like that, but I do keep them at arm's length.

I still have to fight myself sometimes to not expect the worst out of everyone. The guys around me, my brother, they made me see different and that not all men are the same.

When you are betrayed by almost everyone in your life but your siblings? It's hard to understand and get out of that train of thought that is bad.

"Do you want more kids one day?" he asks out of the blue bringing me out of my depressing thoughts.

Without hesitation, I respond, "I would love more kids, Michaela would be the best big sister." I smile at the thought of her helping me take care of a baby.

Tristan lays his head against mine. "She would." It's sweet the way he is lying against me, the way his hand is stroking mine.

It's such a small thing but it's so intimate.

The door to the building opens and we both get out walking to the door to get Michaela.

My friend smiles happily at me. "She did absolutely amazing today. See you in two days?" She upped the time in between appointments so that is a great sign.

I squeeze her hand and look down at Michaela. "I think Tristan wants to ask you something."

She looks at him eyes wide, chomping at the bit to figure out what it is. "How do you feel about trampolines?" he asks nonchalantly.

Her mouth pops open in shock as she connects the dots. "Oh my God, are we going?" she rushes out so fast we barely understand her.

He nods at her smiling.

She jumps on him, he lifts her up and hugs her back just as tight as she hugs him. "This is the best day of my life," she says dramatically.

Tristan of course is eating that shit up, the look on his face is letting me know that she has made his whole entire year.

She is the best person to surprise. Once, a few years ago I wrapped an orange in wrapping paper, then had her open it; she acted like it was the best thing she ever received.

She is my sweet baby.

"COME ON, Mommy. You can do it!" Michaela screams as I stand on top of the wall waiting to drop off into the foam pit to my death.

My worst fear you may ask?

Heights.

I am terrified! If I even think of something high off the ground or the thought of me falling any distance, it frightens me.

Tristan and Michaela jumped off the ledge with absolutely no problems, now I am terrified, trying to talk myself into actually jumping.

I have taken like three running attempts but stopped at the end, not able to do it.

Tristan and Michaela are both sitting at the edge of the pit waiting for me to actually do it.

I close my eyes and step off the ledge, my heart in my throat until I hit the foam blocks sinking completely to the bottom of the pit, to the trampoline under me.

A hand shoots in front of my face taking ahold of my hands, lifting me out of the pit and into Tristan's arms. They are both laughing hysterically at me.

"Mommy, you should have seen your face." Michaela reaches over grabbing ahold of my cheeks squishing them together.

Tristan hugs me tighter, practically dragging me out of the pit and onto the side then lifts out Michaela.

"Tristan, can we do the ninja course?" She points to the obstacle course across the trampoline park.

"Sure."

She stands, jumping up and down excitedly. He helps me off the ground and I wipe off my butt smiling at him.

He is so cute, his hair is slightly messed up from the jumping and it just makes him all the more handsome. The most attractive thing though is the way he is with my baby, he gives her his full attention. I love that.

One way to my heart is through my baby and let me tell you, Tristan is knocking on the door right now.

I follow them over and I notice all of the moms staring at him right now. I don't blame them because I 'm doing the exact same thing.

I sit down on one of the seats for parents so they can keep an eye on their kids. "Come on Michaela, you can beat him." I wink at Tristan who is lifting her off the ground so she can reach the monkey bars.

I 'm so intent on watching them, mostly Tristan from the way his arm muscles are flexing from every movement; it's way hot I have to admit. My eyes are glued to his body, God, he is so sexy.

I don't even notice the person sitting down directly next to me, their thigh touching mine until they speak. "What are you looking at?" a deep voice asks, scaring me badly.

I jump and look over at the voice, kind of mad at myself for being so preoccupied. "Uhh," I say stupidly, because my heart is trying to catch up.

He looks at me, smiling weirdly. I pretend to look in my purse and I scoot over, away from him so he is not touching me.

His hair is perfectly fashioned in style. He's wearing a white button up shirt with black pants and very polished shoes. Kind of a weird way to dress for a trampoline place.

I can feel his eyes on me, it's like he's trying to drill holes into my body with them. "Are you from here?" he asks.

I look at him fully, trying to see if he's trying to be nice or if there's something weird going on.

"I am not." I don't lie.

He tilts his head to the side. "Are you here with your kids?" I ask him.

He smiles. "Nah, I'm not here with anyone. I don't have kids."

A red alert goes off in my head at that. Why would he be here dressed like that unless he was here with someone else?

I look around to make sure Michaela is okay. She is sitting in the pit with Tristan throwing foam blocks at him.

"I have to go; I hope you have a good day," I tell him, picking up my purse and standing up to walk to Tristan.

His hand bands around my forearm, spinning me around hard. "I was not done talking to you, woman." His eyes are dark, I can see the fury he has because I dismissed him.

I connect the dots, the way he is dressed and the way he just spoke to me.

"You are here from the cult," I tell him.

He grins. "Bingo. Now you are going to leave with me, not make a scene or I will hurt your daughter." He looks over my shoulder, I know at Michaela.

My heart beats so hard I can feel it in my throat, I am scared but I am more scared for my baby.

But I know that with Tristan here no one is going to hurt my baby, so I do the most rational thing.

I punch him in the fucking face.

He lets me go and I push back away from him putting some distance between us.

I smell Tristan before I see him. He takes my hand gently, the one that just hit that guy in the face, studies it, running his finger over the knuckles then turns my arm over to look at the red finger marks.

"What are you doing?" I ask him confused.

"Cataloging all the parts of him I am going to break," he says so simply.

He turns to look at the guy who hurt me, his hand shooting out in a split second wrapping around his throat. "Let's go for a little trip." He drags him by his throat, literally to the men's bathroom. "Wait, Tristan," I call.

He turns to look at me. "He is a part of the cult; he threatened to hurt Michaela if I didn't listen to him." I am not ashamed to know that I just signed his death warrant.

I turn around to check on Michaela who is climbing through a tunnel, I am so glad she didn't see this. I sit back down trying to let my heart slow down and try to understand what is happening.

Tristan

I PUSH him hard onto the floor the second we are inside of the men's bathroom. I lock the door behind me so no one can get in.

His face pales at the sound of the lock clicking in place. "Let me leave and you won't get hurt." He stands up, pointing his finger at me like I'm going to be intimidated by this pussy.

I reach forward wrapping my hand around his finger, not moving, letting him try to get free from my grip. His face turns a splotchy red, pulling back until I hear the most satisfying snap.

He screams at the top of his lungs. I laugh even louder loving that he's in pain. I move to his other fingers, breaking them one by one in retaliation for Lynn getting hurt.

I grip the back of his head, my fingers digging deep in his hair making sure to pull.

I bring him over to the toilet, lifting the lid. "Are you going to accept your beating like a man?" Letting him think he may have a chance to get out of this, I ask him knowing that he won't because he's not a man.

He starts to fight me, trying to stand and get away. I sigh, okay then. His fighting is futile, he is hurting himself more than he is me. "She is just a fucking whore, why are you doing this? She doesn't belong to you. She is free game. It was decreed!" he screams like a little girl, trying to push me away from him.

Nothing can change his fate; nothing is going to stop me from killing him. He signed his death warrant when he breathed the same oxygen as my Lynn.

"Decreed huh?" I ask, letting him think that I am listening, that he can talk his way out of his.

He looks at me. "The head pastor has made her, Etta, Michaela, all of the fucking women in the center, free game. We can do what we want without punishment, I needed a new wife. For a whore, she is beautiful." He gets a wistful look on his face thinking of Lynn.

I grin, anger burning through every part of me straight to my core. I want to wrap my hands around every one of those fuckers' throats.

While he is distracted, I press his face onto the dirty fucking floor, grinding it in the shit, piss, and God knows what else is on the floor.

I lift the trash can and dump it into the toilet to make sure it gets clogged up and filled to the top with water.

I lift him and press his face in the water, banging his face into the bottom of the toilet bowl, knowing I've broken something.

A sane person would let him go thinking that he has learned his lesson, but I am not a sane person. Nothing sane about me when it comes to my girls.

I stand there, waiting and waiting until he stops moving. I let him go, leaving him lying in the toilet facedown.

I see a closet inside of the bathroom. I carry him over and throw him inside under a ton of stuff so no one can see him if they do happen to look inside.

I take out my phone and call Techy, the Devil Souls tech guy. "Hey, I just murdered someone in the bathroom of the jump house in your town. Can you erase the footage for me?"

I hear silence for a few seconds. "Wait? Why?" he says but I hear him typing away.

"A fucking cult member hurt Lynn."

I hear him cuss under his breath. "Well, fuck yeah I can. Do you need me to send the prospects to clean up for you?"

"I was going to call my boys, but if you can get them, that would be fucking great."

I walk out of the bathroom and move a cleaning sign in front of it so no one will go in.

"Sure thing, Lynn is family."

"Thanks, man." I hang up the phone finding Lynn standing in the same spot. I can see the worry on her face as I walk up to her.

I pull her into my arms, kissing the top of her head. "Darlin, you okay?" I pick up her sore hand looking at it again to make sure she is okay, the red marks on her skin infuriating me.

She nods against my chest. "I wish they would leave me

alone. It's been so many years; I just don't understand why they keep doing this."

I feel fucking helpless. Every one of my protective instincts is on high alert. I want to destroy fucking everyone and watch them burn.

I look over at Michaela to make sure she is okay, but she is oblivious to all as she plays on the trampolines.

I hear Lynn sniff and I pull her back out of my arms so I can look at her. She looks down at the ground trying to hide the tears from me.

"Hey." I put my finger under her chin, lifting her head so I can look at her beautiful eyes.

"Don't cry, honey." I catch her tears that are sliding down her face and breaking my heart.

She tries to smile at me, her lips trembling too hard for that to happen. I brush my finger over them, hating this.

"I think it's just the adrenaline wearing off is all," she explains.

I pull her into me again, sitting down onto the seat holding her until Michaela's time is up, my eyes not leaving her for a second.

The bell goes off letting us know our time is up; Michaela runs over to us with her shoes. "That was so much fun, Mommy!" She face-plants into Lynn's belly.

The sadness goes from her eyes the instant she is around. "You looked like you had a lot of fun!" She rubs the back of Michaela's head, who then sits down onto the floor putting her sandals back on.

I take Lynn's hand, not wanting her to be far from me and I hold Michaela's in the other. My body is primed and ready to fuck someone up if they even glance at them wrong.

I let my guard down here, that shit won't ever happen again.

On the way out I pass the Devils Prospects going in. I nod at them and they go straight to the bathroom to clean up.

Lynn looks at them in confusion. "I wonder why they are here?" she questions, eyes following them to the bathroom.

I grin. "Just cleaning up some shit I suppose."

She gives me a confused look, but turns her attention to Michaela who is talking a hundred miles a minute about her experience today.

"Who likes seafood boils?" I ask, spotting a seafood restaurant next door.

Michaela clutches her heart. "Crab legs are my life." She holds her hand up in the alien symbol which makes absolutely no sense but it's cute nonetheless.

"I love it," Lynn tells me.

"Well, let me go feed my girls."

Lynn

"LET ME GO FEED MY GIRLS." His words ring over and over in my head, I try to hide the way that made me feel.

But I felt those words, I felt it in every part of me.

I squeeze his hand letting him know that I noticed his words, I don't think I will ever forget them.

The way he played with Michaela today, he gave her his undivided attention and I loved that so much.

The way he pays attention to me too, he notices instantly if something is bothering me, he confronts me.

He protected me today.

I don't know what happened in that bathroom, but I do know that I will never see that person again.

We get to the restaurant and the second they see Tristan with his cut, we are seated instantly in a booth. The perks of being a MC member, you're treated like royalty.

Michaela sits beside me with Tristan in front of us facing the restaurant. We are seated away from everyone, giving us privacy.

Which I need right now.

I am still dealing with the emotions of what just happened earlier, I never expected that.

It truly makes me wonder how many of those cult members are still out there. I do know that we were the start of the fall for them.

I knew we are hated, Etta especially, and that is something we have learned to deal with but seeing it firsthand today, in my face, someone recognized me. It made it more real.

Nothing compares to what happened with Michaela. That was a slap in the face that is still stinging to this very moment.

The waiter comes by with the menus and to take our drink orders. Tristan points out some huge meals for all of us to share.

Michaela has found her bib on the table and I help her tie it around her neck and her hair into a bun.

"I hope you know, the lady in us goes right out the window when it comes to seafood," I point out.

He laughs. "Darlin, you could have four eyes and I would still think you are beautiful."

Michaela puts her hand under her face staring at him. "Aww, Tristan! That was nice."

He is really nice. He scoots forward and takes her little hand. "You are beautiful too, little lady."

She beams like he just gave her the best present in the world. "Thank you kind sir, me and mother appreciate it," she says in her British accent that she tried to do.

I laugh and Tristan joins me, I can see the happiness on his face when he looks at both of us.

With the shit happening all around me, these moments mean the most.

When the waiter comes back, he orders one of the biggest

boils on the menu for all of us to share. Michaela is practically bouncing in her seat at the prospect of feasting on crab legs.

"Mom, when do I go back to school?" she asks, taking a sip of her water.

I think on it for a moment. "Next week if you're feeling up to it?"

She puts her hands together. "I know I have a game next week is all." She gives me puppy eyes. "You can go as long as you want to," I tell her.

I just don't want to push her too much into anything. I want her to adjust to everything that has happened, but she is dealing with things way better than I ever imagined.

The food is brought in by two waiters since one can't carry it all. They set the bag onto the table opening it for us.

Michaela is practically drooling looking at the food. "Can I start, Tristan?" she asks him for permission.

"Go right ahead, princess."

She gives him the happiest smile at him calling her princess but then we are totally ignored as she starts cracking the crab legs.

I dig in myself, closing my eyes at the amazing sauce they have for the seafood. A few minutes pass before Tristan speaks again.

"So, I wanted to ask you something very important, Michaela." Tristan looks over at me before turning back to her. She puts her crab leg down giving him her full attention.

Her little brow is furrowed as she is confused and so am I. "I wanted to get your blessing sweetheart to take your mom out on a date."

Her little mouth pops open in an O shape, she looks at me then at him before smacking her hands together. "Oh my gosh! You have to wear a suit and get her flowers. It's a must."

He sits back like he was just told the best thing ever, me on the other hand? I am floored. That was the sweetest, most thoughtful thing he could have done.

He knows how important she is to me and for him to ask her? That means so much to me.

"How about this? Tomorrow evening, me and you go out before I go out with your mom, if she is okay with that?" he suggests.

A little piece of my heart flies out of my chest and into him. "It's more than fine with me." My heart is so full.

8

TRISTAN

THE NEXT DAY

"WE WILL BE BACK LATER, MOMMY!" Michaela runs over to her mom, giving her a hug before running to me, taking my hand.

Lynn walks over to me, giving me a hug, her head resting on my chest for a second. Fuck, my heart.

"You guys have a great time together." I touch her cheek, smiling at her. "Lock the door behind us, a prospect is at the gate." I nod my head in the direction of where he is sitting.

Michaela opens the door, more than ready for an evening out. Ever since I mentioned it, she has gone over and over what we could do together.

I do have a surprise for her.

I lift her into her seat, buckling her in. I get in and start the truck and she points her finger at me. "Play us some jams." Then turns her fingers into a rock symbol.

I chuckle, she is the funniest kid I have ever met. Just to be around her makes you happy.

I turn on the radio to a country station. "I do like some George." She nods her head to the music.

A little while later we pull up to the new store that just

opened in town; it's basically a little girl's heaven. I passed it a few days ago coming into town.

I pull up in front, her eyes are large taking in the pink store with princesses and other girly things on the front of the building.

"Oh my gosh what is this place?!" she whisper yells as I help her out of the seat. I take her hand leading her into the store.

"Hi! What can I do for you guys?" A lady walks up to us.

I see on the wall different packages. "Let's do the deluxe, this little girl needs to be spoiled."

I can see the dollar signs in the saleslady's eyes. "Well then! First things first, let's go pick out your outfit, princess."

Michaela practically floats after her into a room full of princess dresses and dolls. "Now, you pick out your dress and the doll you want so we can get her dressed in a matching outfit."

She turns away from the saleslady, to look at me her eyes full of tears. "Tristan, this is the best day of my life!" She runs to me, smashing her face in my belly.

I bend down onto my knees and hug her tight. "Sweet girl, you deserve it. You and your momma both do." I kiss her little forehead.

I lean back, wiping away her little tears, her little freckles shining. "Now, go pick out the dress you want. You have some pampering to do, sweetheart."

She flashes me her little toothless grin and she runs to the wall with all of the beautiful dresses.

I sit down on a small ass chair for little kids that holds a tea party set. The look of wonder on her face as she inspects every single dress is incredible. She finds a yellow one, then gets her shoes and tiara. She is sat in a chair where they do her hair for her.

Once she is done, she walks over to me turning in circles. "Wow, you look so beautiful, princess."

She beams at me, then shows me her brand-new doll. "Do we get a castle for her?" She points to a huge castle type play-house for her dolls.

"Do you want that too?" I ask her as she sits down next to me.

I am sure I am going overboard, but I can't help it. I just want to shower Michaela with love in any way possible.

Her eyes widen in shock that I am even offering. "It's a lot of money, Tristan."

"Darlin, if you want it? You can have it." I take her little hand, rubbing the back of it.

She stands up so fast her chair falls back against the floor. She lays into my chest. "I love you, Tristan."

My poor fucking heart, it was just ripped out of my chest by a small little girl. I close my eyes and pull her into my lap, holding her as long as she will let me.

"I love you too, sweet girl." I rub her back.

Hearing her say those words to me, I never fucking dreamed I would hear them.

"Alright here is your dinner, princess." One of the workers interrupts the moment, putting small sandwiches and other small foods onto the table.

Michaela smiles at her. "Why thank you, kind lady!" she says in that very proper voice of hers.

"She wants the castle dollhouse too." I point over at the castle and the lady practically screams with excitement.

I turn my attention to Michaela who is holding her drink in her hand, with her pinky in the air. "This is a fine dinner don't you think, prince Tristan?" she says to me.

I try not to laugh at her fake accent. "It sure is."

She pours me some tea. "You need a crown prince Tristan, let me grab you one, kind sir." She runs across the store and grabs a crown, plopping it on my head.

She steps back, her hands on her hips. "Now that is much better." She sits back down and eats her little sandwiches.

I smile at her, listening to her ramble random facts about the Disney princesses. I think a surprise trip to Disney is in order.

The time flies by. They are delivering her dollhouse tomorrow since the one in the store is just for show.

I take her hand and walk to the flower shop next door. "Let's get some flowers, shall we?"

She skips the whole way, still in her brand-new dress and tiara. She is so cute. I open the door for her and she walks inside, looking around the store.

Lynn

IMAGINE MY SURPRISE when as soon as Tristan left, Lani knocks on my door, letting herself in with a makeup case and a dress over her arm.

"Did I forget something today?" I'm confused as to why she is here.

She smiles widely. "Darlin, Tristan sent me here. He told me to pamper you before your date tonight."

I swoon, how thoughtful is he?

She takes my hand and drags me upstairs. "Get in the shower while I get set up."

I get in the shower, making sure to shave everything as nerves settle into my belly.

What are we doing tonight?

This is my first date, ever. I was just married overnight. I don't know how to do all of this; I am so far from normal with a lot of baggage. No, I don't mean my daughter, I mean emotionally.

I'm healed but I'm afraid of having a PTSD attack, because I want to have a real relationship. I want to be with Tristan. He makes me happy and it's unreal to even think of how we met and everything that has happened since. I am surprised by how much I feel for him in such a short time span.

But he has proved to me over and over how much he wants to be here, how much he cares for Michaela.

I know that he truly cares for me. I let the worry and the nervousness wash away because this is Tristan. I am safe with him.

Stepping out of the shower, I wrap myself in a towel walking into my bedroom. "Sit here while I blow dry your hair."

Tristan texted Lani letting her know that he is on his way back. "I ', so nervous," I admit to Lani.

She laughs. "Trust me, I know the feeling. I was so nervous when it came to Vinny and Trey." She smiles at me softly. "Tristan is your person, the second he saw you? There was no one else. He looks at you the way my guys look at me."

I can't even breathe. "What do you mean?" I ask breathlessly.

"Like he would kill anyone and everyone who dared to take you from him."

Oh shit.

"I am so happy for you, Trey, and my brother. The way you guys love each other is amazing and I have seen it over the years. You fought for me and Etta all of those years ago, you were going to take us with you even if Vinny didn't want to. I 'm so thankful for you." My eyes mist over, her reflection going blurry in the mirror.

Lani wraps her arms around me from behind. I squeeze her arms, both of us just hugging each other.

The doorbell rings and we both jump the moment breaking. I admire myself in the mirror and slip on my heels. "How do I look?" I ask Lani one last time, running my hands down my sides.

"Beautiful." She hugs me and pushes me toward the door. "Go have fun! Michaela will be fine with us tonight."

I walk down the stairs; I can see them both standing outside of the door. I pull it open.

Both of them are standing there holding a bouquet of flowers, Michaela is decked out in princess attire and Tristan. WOW. Tristan is dressed in boots, jeans, and a button up shirt.

"Wow, you look absolutely beautiful." Tristan reaches forward taking my hand to kiss the back of it.

I blush at the compliment. "Thank you, you look really handsome yourself," I point out.

He smiles and hands me my flowers. "These are beautiful Tristan, thank you."

I turn my attention to my sweet girl. "Wow!! Who is this beautiful princess?!"

She grins at me. "Look Mommy, Tristan got me some flowers too! He said I was his princess."

I turn around to look at Lani who looks like she is ready to pass out like I am. "Wow, you are mine too!"

She grins even wider. "I am everyone's."

I press a kiss to her forehead. "Yes, you are angel, have a nice night with Lani." I pull her into a tight hug. It's so hard to leave her.

"If you need mommy, I will come and get you anytime. Okay?" I tell her.

She nods. "I know, have fun!" She takes my hand and puts it in Tristan's hand. I take that as my cue to leave.

I wave over my shoulder to the both of them. Tristan opens his truck door helping me inside. He leans over me, taking the seat belt and buckling me in.

I inhale sharply at the heat and the closeness of his body. God, he looks so good right now.

"Got to keep my girl safe." He gives me a wicked grin.

I swear he knows what he does to me. He shuts the door and I let out a deep breath dying on the inside.

He gets in and I take a second to admire him again. He looks really amazing and he has put a lot of thought into today.

"Thank you for what you did with Michaela, she is so happy."

"She is an amazing little girl, she 's very special." He turns to look at me, "Just like her mom. "

There goes my heart once again out of the window. "You are so kind to the both of us."

He slows down and looks at me for a second before turning back to the road. "You deserve all of the fucking kindness and good things in your life, sweetheart."

I reach over and take his hand, intertwining our fingers. I need to be close to him right now.

I catch his small smile at me making the first move. He pulls up in front of a fancy restaurant in town which I have never been to before.

I open my door to step out but he reaches across me, pulling my door shut. "Oh no, I got your door."

He walks around to my door and opens it, then I think how am I going to get out without flashing everyone. Tristan reaches one arm behind my back and the other under my legs, he sets me gently onto the ground.

"Thank you." I smile.

He puts his hand on the small of my back, leading me inside. "Walker," he tells the hostess and we're led to a private booth toward the back of the restaurant.

"I thought Walker was your dad's name?" I question as I sit down in the booth, he sits down beside me instead of across from me.

"Walker is our last name, but everyone calls him Walker."

"Ohh okay, that makes sense."

He opens the menu putting it in front of both of us to share. "My dad was a single dad, he raised me entirely by himself. He stayed single up until a few years ago when he met Aiden's mom but they only dated a few months."

"That's amazing, your dad raised such an amazing guy." I squeeze his knee.

"My friend is wanting to prospect for the club and he is coming to stay with my dad until he can find a house. I would love for you to meet them both."

I lean my head on his shoulder for a minute. "I would love that."

He kisses me on the top of my head. "I think I want a steak, what do you want?" he asks, lifting the menu for me to see. "I think I will get the same. "

"This is my first date, ever," I admit to him once the waiter leaves with our order.

He smirks at me. "I can't admit that I am not glad for that, I am a selfish man when it comes to you."

Well, fuck me sideways, that was hot.

"I see." I arch an eyebrow at him. The waiter sets my glass of wine in front of me. "Now how long has it been since you've been on a date?" I ask him.

He winks, putting his hand on my bare knee. "Darlin, I was a teenager in high school. I'm completely reserved for you." He scoots closer, moving until his lips are inches away from me. "All of me."

"Oh, fuck me," I gasp, my body is on fire at his words.

He licks his lips. "Just say the words, angel." He presses his lips against mine, stealing what air I have left in my body, claiming it as his own.

Time stands still around us; it's just us and the way he makes me feel right now. His hand is still on my knee, my body is way too aware of that.

I am dying for him to bring it further up, I want him to love me the way I should be loved. To be loved the way his lips are touching mine right now.

His fingers move gently across my knee and I shiver at the

contact. I pull back because I am so close to embarrassing myself.

He kisses the side of my lip, before turning back around in the seat taking a long pull of his beer.

I can't resist the urge to peek in his lap to see if he is as affected as I am. I look down slightly and back up before he catches me but I still didn't get a look so I do it again.

"What are you doing?" he asks.

I die inside, I wish the ground would swallow me up. "Nothing," I stutter, taking a drink of my wine trying to play it off.

He bursts out laughing, it's so loud and I know people are staring at us. My face is so hot, I'm sure I'm going to die.

"Oh baby." He reaches over and hugs me to him. "You're the cutest thing I have ever fucking seen. If you want to look at my dick, I can give you a first-hand look."

Yeah, I am going to do die. That is a fact.

"Tristan," I groan, covering my face with my hands, I'm so embarrassed.

He laughs again, he doesn't make a sound but I can feel his body moving with it. "Look at me."

I slowly peek up at him through my eyelashes, still wanting to hide. "I am sorry I embarrassed you, baby. If you're wondering if I was turned on, I have been every fucking day since I met you." I look at him fully. "I'm fucking obsessed with you."

The embarrassment leaves me in a flash, leaving me wanting him even more. I lean my head over into the crook of his neck. "I'm obsessed with you too."

And I am, I have never once wanted someone in my life until him. No one else have I gave a second thought to.

"Fuck, yeah," he says lowly.

I can still feel eyes on us, but I don't care.

Lynn

AFTER DINNER, I fully expected him to bring us home but he pulls to a stop outside of a country bar.

"What are we doing here?" I ask.

He reaches into the back seat and pulls out a pair of cowboy boots. "Darlin, we are going dancing."

He gets out, walking around the truck opening my door. "Turn around, sweetheart."

He gently slips my heels off my feet, he sets them onto the floor. He rubs his thumb up the middle of my foot, giving me a slight massage. I close my eyes at the incredible sensation. He moves to the other foot, giving it the same amount of attention.

"Once we are home, I will give you a better massage." He reaches inside one of the shoes and takes out a brand-new pair of socks.

He slowly puts the socks on my feet, dragging them up above my ankles and slips the boots on for me.

"You are so good to me, Tristan. I have never experienced this before," I admit, emotional.

"Fuck, baby." He wraps his arm around my back lifting me out of the truck, slamming his lips against mine.

All of the kisses we've shared before have been soft, sweet, and so full of emotion but this one is fiery and it burns me from deep within.

His tongue strokes against mine, I grip his shoulders needing something to ground me.

"Fuck, your kisses I can never grow tired of," he mumbles against my lips before settling me on my wobbly feet.

His arm doesn't leave my back. "You ready?"

I smile. "Ready."

The inside of the bar is dark, filled with a bunch of lights flashing all around the crowd and it's smokey and the music is so loud I can feel it in my chest.

Tristan leads me straight to the dance floor, he presses my chest against his front, his hand moving down my back, slowly down my ass. My eyes stare into his, waiting to see what he is going to do.

He grips the edge of my dress, dragging it further down my legs. "I can't let anyone see what is mine."

He just wrecked me.

"Yours, huh?" I question, trying to play it off.

He licks his beautiful lips, his eyes piercing straight into mine. "You are definitely mine, all of you is."

His hand rubs across my ass, before settling on my back. "Now, let me show you how I dance."

His hand moves to my hip, putting his leg in between mine and he moves my body exactly the way he wants it, leading me across the dance floor. I have never felt so alive in my life, his eyes staring straight into my soul. If someone even dares to get close to me, he stares them down and they get the hint.

He is branding me as his own and he is not just telling everyone around us.

No, he is telling me too.

The thing is I want to be his.

———

Hours later, we are both exhausted. We walk out of the bar, Tristan holding me against his side.

The cool night air feels great on my skin. "God, that was such fun. We have to do it again soon." I smile up at him.

We didn't drink anymore tonight. We didn't need it to have fun. "Should we make Friday nights our date night?" He pats my ass slightly.

"For a disciple girl, you sure aren't acting like it." I hear a man yell out across the parking lot.

Fear hits me hard. The parking lot is completely empty

except for us and someone in the dark.

Tristan is staring into the dark off into the tree line. He pushes me gently behind him putting his body in between me and the person who just yelled. Tristan doesn't say anything back, he just stares into the dark waiting for the person to show themselves.

Then out of the darkness three men step out into the parking lot. "It seems to me that you're a jezebel in the flesh; I saw the way you were tempting the men in there with your flesh."

It's someone from the cult. How did they find me again?

"You need to come with us so I can save you from your sinning ways." The leader of the group moves closer to us. "I do need that bounty money too."

Wait, bounty? How did that happen and why me?

"Lynn, get in the truck."

I don't want to leave Tristan to face all of these men alone so I take ahold of his hand, scared. They move closer to us, around ten feet away. Tristan doesn't take his eyes off of them. My heart feels like it could explode out of my chest, my skin is tingling from being scared.

I can't resist the urge to ask what they mean by that; they aren't looking at Tristan. No, they are staring at me like I am their meal ticket.

Tristan takes my hand, pulling me closer to him. "A bounty?" I question, hoping they will answer me.

The leader of the group, is dressed just like all of the cult members in brown khaki pants and a white button up shirt, their hair perfectly styled. He steps a little closer, looking at me like I am the scum beneath his feet. "Do you not know?"

Tristan tightens his hand on mine, his hand is shaking in mine. I know his isn't the fear, no, this is anger. It's radiating off him in waves.

The men won't look at him, they are looking at me. I am not

a person to them. "You killed Lee, he and Gavin are the grand-sons of Danielson."

It hits me like a ton of bricks as to the severity of this; Danielson is the leader of the whole clan.

Fuck.

He smirks at me, knowing I 'm catching the meaning of it all. "Michaela is Gavin's future wife and you are keeping her from him. The punishment for that?" He stops talking, looking at me like he is so happy. "Is your death. So, we are all called to bring you in and bring your daughter in. We will be heroes! Oh and if we bring in that bitch Etta? We will never have to work again in our lives."

My knees start to buckle at the mention of Michaela. I will go underground with her if I have to. They are never ever going to get her; I'd rather die.

"Get in the truck, Lynn," Tristan tells me again, looking at me for a split second. I want to argue, but I do as he asks opening the door to the truck.

"Hey come back here!" one of the guys yells. I climb inside and shut the door just as someone comes from behind the truck grabbing ahold of the door handle.

Tristan pulls him back by his hair, away from the truck and I lock the doors just as someone bangs into the side of it again.

His face comes into view in front of me, banging onto the glass trying to break in. I stare into the face of the person who I have never met before, but the way they are looking at me is someone who truly hates me for protecting my daughter.

I hear a man yell, screaming at the top of his lungs. I turn my focus from the man trying to get into the window, hitting it with his fists, rocks, whatever he can.

Headlights shine in the window directly at me, blinding me. I try to cover my eyes to see what is going on when the car with the lights shining on me, starts squealing moving straight at me.

Oh my God.

9

TRISTAN

I HEAR SQUEALING tires and I spin around, pushing the fucker off of me that is trying to climb on my back like a pussy.

The car is going straight toward Lynn.

Fuck.

I take my gun out of the back of my pants, pointing it at the car and shooting in the direction of the driver hoping that I can hit him before he hits Lynn.

Fuck! Fuck! It repeats over and over in my head the closer it gets. I can't fucking bear to look at Lynn right now.

Just as he reaches her, another fucking truck comes out of nowhere, t-boning it on the driver's side pushing it out of the way before it could hit my truck.

I put my gun to the head of the fucker who is trying to fight me, I don't even blink or hesitate pulling the trigger ending him. This shit is over.

I grab the fucker who is the leader of this fucking cult and shove him to the ground. I push his face onto the pavement, dragging him by his hair loving that the skin is getting ripped off his face.

He's screaming at the top of his lungs and I chuckle, the darkness in me coming out full force.

They threatened her. They wanted to hurt her. I will never fucking forget this.

"What's the matter you fucking pussy? Not so brave now, are you?" I pick his face up slamming it back down onto the pavement.

Blood is pouring from his nose onto the ground, I turn him around wanting him to drown in it.

"I 'm not going to let you die, no. You are going back to your leader and you are going to tell him that he is a fucking dead man. Tell him the Sinners are coming for him."

I lift his hand, bending back his fingers one by one, staring him dead in the eyes, smiling, wanting him to see that he is my bitch and I will destroy him. He screams over and over, drowning in the blood pouring down the back of his throat.

I do the same to the other hand, taking my time, making him suffer. The words "wanting to kill Lynn", that broke something in me, the dark side of myself that I keep locked away.

He is out and he is ready to fucking murder everyone.

Lynn

I WATCH RIGHT before my very eyes as Tristan tortures someone; the screams he's bringing from that man would give a normal person nightmares.

Not me.

I want them all to suffer for everything they are doing to Michaela.

Tristan picks him up and slams him back onto the ground once more, his head bouncing off the pavement with a sickening thud.

I scream as a face comes in front of the window, scaring me. He has a gun pointing it right at me.

Oh my God.

I back further away from the window, toward the driver's side wanting to put as much distance as I can away from him.

He mouths to me, "Get out of the truck, or I will kill you." He waves the gun at me.

No way in hell am I getting out of the truck, so I do the only thing I can. I raise my middle finger, flipping him off.

I see the fire in his eyes, the anger at me. He takes off the safety of the gun, I swallow hard. The truck is bulletproof but the fear is still there.

A head pops up behind him and Tristan puts his own gun to his head pulling the trigger, killing the guy. I hear his body hitting the ground through the window.

With shaking hands, I crawl back over to the passenger seat, unlocking the door. He rips it open lifting me out of the truck, pulling me into his arms. "Oh God, I was so scared for you," I mumble against his chest.

"Shh, no need to be scared for me, baby. I have you." He kisses the top of my head.

"Well, isn't this sweet?"

Tristan sets me on my feet and places me behind him so quickly, it's a blur. "Fuck, Darren! That was you? It's good to see you, brother," Tristan says and walks over to the guy and does the guy hand shaking hug thing.

Tristan turns to me, lifting out his hand wanting me to come to him. I do, taking ahold of his hand. "This is Darren, we have served together for years. The one I mentioned at dinner earlier."

I smile at him. "It's nice to meet you. Thank you for saving our butts and all."

He smiles at me. I would have to be blind to not admit that

he is an attractive guy. "Well, I think my truck might be totaled." He laughs like it's no big deal.

Tristan winces when he looks over at it. "Well, I will get one of the guys at the garage to fix it for you. We can drop you off at dad's on the way back."

"Sounds good." He looks at me then at Tristan, I know he's trying to figure out what is happening.

"I do want to know what the fuck is happening and why there is one man an inch from death and others dead." Darren looks all around the mess that we have caused.

"I will explain on the way to dad's." Tristan puts his phone away; he was texting someone. "I have prospects coming to clean all of this shit up."

Tristan lifts me inside the truck, putting my seat belt on me. Darren gets in the back.

What a freaking evening. I just wanted to have an amazing date with Tristan and it comes to this.

Tristan gets in and blasts the heat. "You okay, baby?" he asks me.

I nod. "I'm okay, it just shocked me is all. Still is the best date I ever had," I tell him and he laughs. "Good to know, baby."

Tristan looks in the mirror at Darren then explains everything that's happening. I tune it out not wanting a reminder of how fucked up everything is.

I just want my life to be normal.

"You need to tell Konrad about the bounty, they have one on Etta too," I remind Tristan.

I"m the one they want; they are blaming me for Lee's death. A death I know that he deserved.

Lee, he tricked all of us. He took his kid to school so he could befriend us, just to get my daughter.

The drive to Walker's house is long because it's another town over. We pull up in front of a huge brick house that is close the Grim Sinners club house.

"Darren, it was really nice to meet you. Maybe you can come over for dinner sometime?" I ask.

He smiles at me softly. "I would like that, darlin."

I catch Tristan's glare when he calls me darlin. I hide my smile and Darren winks at me letting me know he said it on purpose.

Walker walks out of his house, walking to Tristan and Darren. I reach over and cover myself with Tristan's jacket feeling cold.

Walker looks over in my direction and moves over to me. I sit up straight dying inside that he's seeing me after all of this happened.

I have met Walker before but this is different because I'm with Tristan now.

He pulls open my door and looks at me. "Hi sweetheart, you feeling okay?" he asks, leaning back against the door.

He looks so much like Tristan; they both have those kind eyes but Walker is more rough, ragged and you can see he has seen some shit in his life. Don't get me wrong, the Grim Sinners are badass but the OGs are a different breed before they built it from the ground up.

I smile at him, the nervousness gone from seeing Tristan in his eyes. "Yeah, I'm fine, what a mess huh?"

His face softens. "Yea that's some shit, isn't it honey? But don't you worry, your father-in-law will get shit handled." My heart stops a little at that. He winks and backs away. "Next time you bring that sweet little girl of yours over so I can see my grandbaby."

I 'm stunned; he just killed me. I'm dead, gone, and destroyed.

He laughs slightly, shutting the door leaving me to thoughts.

Holy fuck.

Tristan doesn't even look apologetic; I know he heard the conversation between us because he was staring at us.

I study Tristan and I really dig deep asking myself. Do I really care?

No, I do not.

I FALL asleep on Tristan on the way back home, my head resting on his thigh. Honestly, the second he ran his fingers through my hair I was asleep.

"Sweetheart, we are home." He wakes me up gently, rubbing my arm.

I yawn and sit up, looking through the window and we are indeed home. I feel much better after that short nap.

I see a small cut on his eyebrow where one of the guys must have hit him. "Are you okay?" I asks, touching beside it.

He takes ahold of my hand gently, the one touching his eyebrow. "I am more than okay."

My stomach flips from the way he is looking at me, I am so blessed with him. He smiles sliding out of the truck, taking me with him, carrying me bridal style into my house.

He carries me straight upstairs to my bedroom, setting me on the edge of the bed. "I 'm going to go shower, get snacks and we can watch movies all night, okay?" he suggests.

I love that idea. "Sounds great, Tristan."

He kisses me on the cheek, leaving me to myself. I grab a long nightshirt of mine, before getting in the shower myself.

I let the water wash down my aching back. My back tends to tense up really bad when I am extremely stressed.

I turn off the water after I wash my hair and body and when I return to my bedroom Tristan is already there with snacks and waters.

"I think you're trying to spoil me."

He winks. "Is it working?"

I laugh and sit down next to him, pulling the blanket over my legs. "It is definitely working."

The only light in the room is the small lamp in the corner. "I am sorry for everything that happened tonight, baby."

I lean over and rest my head against his shoulder. "It's not your fault, it's theirs."

"I know, but you being in any danger at all fucks with me."

Feeling emotional, I raise up, being bold and kiss him. I make the first move, just wanting to stop thinking about all of the bad things and wanting to be here, in the moment with Tristan.

His hands immediately go to my face, touching me so gently, taking over the kiss for me.

I get lost in the feelings of the moment; I need him as much as my next breath.

I lean back, he follows me until he's practically lying on top of me. I can hear the chips and other items falling off the bed onto the floor.

He breaks the kiss, looking down at me. "You are so beautiful, baby," he says in a hushed tone.

I smile as I run my finger over his beautiful lips. "You are beautiful."

He chuckles at my words then shifts slightly so he's lying in between my legs and that's when I feel him. Oh God. His eyes flare, I bite my lip trying not to move as bad as I want to. I want him so bad, I want him in a way I have never wanted anyone before.

He presses his lips against mine again, my hands are shaking against his arms that are braced on either side of my face.

He grows harder against me. I can feel him against my underwear and he is huge. I lift my leg higher not even thinking about it, bringing him even closer. I ache for him to fill me.

His hand takes ahold of my calf, lifting it higher and I gasp breaking the kiss, when he presses against me tighter.

"Darlin, you need to be honest with me. What do you want? If you want me to stop, I will let you go and we can watch movies all night."

His words confirm my answer. "I want you more than anything."

He smiles so happily. "You have me, always."

He grips the bottom of my shirt, lifting it over my head leaving me in just my underwear. Nerves hit me full force, this is so much more intimate that I have ever experienced before. I lift my arms covering myself as he takes off his shirt.

I'm shaking so hard. I'm so nervous, scared, and so excited at the same time. Without a doubt I want to do this.

"Baby, don't hide yourself from me." He takes my hands, pulling them gently to my sides.

"Sorry."

I don't know how to do this; I don't know how to be normal. "I can just look at you all day, you are the most beautiful thing I have ever seen." His fingers trail down my bare sides, leaving goosebumps in their wake.

He sits back, looking down at me, his hands moving to my thighs, down my legs and feet. His eyes never leaving mine the whole time. "I can tell you're scared. I am so fucking sorry baby that someone put that fear in your eyes."

My eyes fill with tears, because he understands.

I want him more than anything but the old thoughts that creep up; what I had before was just pain, hurt, and humiliation. Nothing like this, nothing like Tristan.

No one has looked at me like this, took the time to make sure I was okay.

"I am not scared of you. I have never done this before like this. I never had someone who cares," I tell him honestly, feeling so vulnerable right now. "I want you more than anything, trust me. You're special to me, Tristan."

He puts his hand over his heart, rubbing. "You're so fucking special to me, I more than care about you, Lynn."

He lifts my hand, replacing his. "This is yours. The second you looked at me with those beautiful eyes, I was so gone for you."

I smile widely, the fear gone instantly. "Tristan," I whisper, knowing no words can express how I truly feel right now.

He smiles back at me and I can see in his eyes how he feels about me. I sit up, moving until we are just inches apart. "I want you to make love to me, Tristan. I want you to make me yours."

I can see the fire in his eyes when I mentioned making me his. "With fucking honor."

I sit back, gripping his pants, bringing them down his hips exposing him to me. My mouth waters at the sight of him, so thick, so beautiful. I want to wrap my mouth around him.

Tristan stares down at me, inches from him. I start to wrap my hand around him, but he stops me.

"Right now, it's about you. Lean back, baby."

I lean back into the pillows and he licks his lips staring at me. "All mine," he growls, his hands running down my sides.

He moves over my body and I lift my legs thinking that this is it.

"Oh no baby, we are going to have some fun first."

I give him a questioning look. He kisses me on my lips once more before turning my head to the side, kissing me.

Oh fuck.

He blows across my neck. I run my hands across his bare back, shivers from the goosebumps breaking out across my neck.

"Hmm," he mumbles, moving further down my neck.

He has my face in his grip, not letting me go, controlling me. I 'm soaking wet already and he hasn't even touched me.

He kisses the hollow of my neck, his eyes staring up at me

with every moment. He moves right over my heart, pressing a kiss there. "I can hear how much you want me."

He trails his tongue down in between my breasts before circling back around, closing his mouth around my nipple, sucking.

"Oh God!" The pleasure is shooting straight down to my dripping pussy.

He moves to the other, giving it the same amount of attention. His hand trails down my side, over my belly and stops right before he touches me. He looks at me, I nod knowing that he's asking for permission.

He grips the sides of my underwear tearing each side and throwing it in the floor.

That was way too fucking hot.

Oh God this is really happening.

His fingers slowly glide through my folds, over my clit. His nose flares. "Fuck, you're soaked. We can't let that go to waste."

He sits up, sliding down the bed until he's on his belly in front of me. He slowly puts his finger in his mouth, sucking. "Mm, I needed a little taste."

Fuck me.

This is my first time doing this. He kisses my inner thighs before throwing them over his shoulders and I just hang on for the ride.

His eyes pierce my soul just as he drags his tongue through my folds. "Oh God." I feel pleasure unlike anything I have ever felt before.

"Watch me make you fall apart."

I swear I almost fall apart just from his words. I grip the blankets next to me, my breathing labored as I try to hold back my moans.

I am on fire.

He grins before sucking my clit deep into his mouth, he lets me go before licking his lips and really diving in. "Hmm so good." He kisses my inner thigh before moving back to me with a new vigor.

My toes curl, my whole body freezing, just aching and wanting a little more. He snakes his arm under his chest before he slips a finger inside of me gently. His eyes on me, I know he's making sure I'm okay before he adds another.

"You're so close." He nips me, curling his fingers at the same time and I fall over the edge.

"FUUUUUCK," I scream, my body not my own right now; I'm shaking all the way to my feet.

"Fucking beautiful." Tristan rubs my inner thighs as I come to my senses.

I lean forward and pull him to me, wanting him close right now. This was a huge moment for me; I allowed myself to be vulnerable in a way that I thought I never could be.

I open my legs, settling him in between. "We can stop now," he suggests, kissing my forehead.

"Love me, Tristan," I whisper, his eyes so beautiful as he looks down at me.

"You got it, baby."

"I'm on birth control and I'm clean." I throw it out there when he starts to get off the bed. "So am I," he tells me and settles back against me.

"I feel like I'm fucking dreaming." His hand touches my face, like he is making sure I am real. "It's hard to believe you are mine." He kisses me so sweetly.

His hand snakes in between our bodies, his finger rubbing my clit. I cry out into his mouth and he just continues to kiss me until I am on the brink of coming again.

He breaks the kiss, resting his forehead against mine and lifts my arms above my head intertwining our fingers.

He presses against my entrance. I relax as he slowly slips inside of me, his eyes never leaving mine. I know it's his way of making sure I am okay.

I moan loudly, the burning feeling of being filled. "God." I lift my head kissing him.

He pushes all the way inside of me in one final push. I break the kiss throwing my head back. I feel so full.

He kisses my neck. "God, you feel amazing, Tristan," I moan, squeezing his hands that are on either side of my face.

He kisses my cheek and then my lips, as he starts to move. "You are so beautiful, my girl."

My heart isn't my own anymore, it belongs to him.

"Tristan," I whisper, feeling so emotional and overwhelmed.

His eyes never leave mine as he makes love to me, tenderly, so full of emotions, so full of everything.

My legs are shaking as I get closer and closer to falling apart. My toes curl under, gripping his hips in a death grip as he moves over and over inside of me.

"I can't." I don't even know what I am saying, my eyes closed tightly as I ride out everything I am feeling, it's so overwhelming.

I am on fire.

"Come for me," he growls in my ear, biting the lobe gently and I feel his finger rubbing my clit, pinching and that's all it takes for me to fall.

"Tristan," I moan, digging my nails into his back, arching into him, clenching onto him in a death grip.

He curses as he comes just as hard as I do, both of us out of breath. I kiss his cheek, then his lips softly. He tucks his head into the side of my neck, still buried inside of me.

His hand rubs my hip and thigh. "Are you okay?" he lifts his head, asking. He has such a content look on his face.

I nod. "I am so more than okay, Tristan." My heart is so full it almost hurts. "You are so much more than I ever expected." I rub my thumbs across his cheekbones, his eyes watching. "You came into my life when I least expected it, but I can't imagine life without you in it." I lay myself out bare for him.

"Fuck, angel," he says under his breath, shaking his head. I know my words affected him, but it's the way I feel.

I feel safe with him in a way that I can be completely vulnerable without a single worry.

"You make me so happy; I feel so safe with you." I snuggle deeper into his arms, loving the way he makes me feel.

My biggest worry in life was that when I met someone, I was scared that I could never truly and fully be with someone again.

He took those worries and demolished them; he gave me a part of myself that I thought I would never have.

He cups my face gently. "I would protect you with my life, I would fucking die for you."

Fuck.

He kisses me once more, sliding out of me gently. I wince slightly, sore. He walks into the bathroom, coming back out with a washcloth in his hand.

He steps beside me, pulling my legs open and does the most raw, unexpected thing.

He cleans me.

"Tristan." Tears fill my eyes, dripping onto my cheek. He throws the cloth into the bathroom scooping me up in his arms, holding me. "Those tears in your eyes fucking wreck me."

I laugh slightly, wiping them off my cheeks. "You are just so good to me. I get emotional sometimes."

He grumbles, "Well I still don't fucking like it."

I shake my head smiling. "Well, I will try better," I joke.

His hand comes down, smacking my ass leaving a slight sting. "You better," he states.

I sit up. "Oh yea?? And what are you going to about it?" I tease, licking my lips.

"Ohhh, I can show you." He picks me up suddenly, lying me across his lap, my bare ass up in the air.

I kick my legs trying to push myself off his lap, laughing. He rubs his hand across my bare ass cheek, then he lifts it and whack!

"Hey!" I yell, laughing, wiggling myself in his lap, trying to make him drop me.

Smack!

"Ohh what's this in here?" His hand sneaks between my legs, slipping a finger inside of me. "Ohh someone liked that." He lazily slides his fingers in and out of me, curling them.

"I think you're trying to kill me," I groan, resting my face onto the bed. "I'm at your mercy."

"That's what I like to hear." His voice is rough as his fingers bring me closer and closer to the edge.

I grip the blanket hard, biting it. I am so sensitive from coming twice already. "Fuck! Fuck!" I scream, clenching down hard onto his fingers.

"God, like a fucking vise."

One second I am lying on my stomach, the next I am on my back with his mouth sucking my clit into his mouth, his fingers buried deep.

"FUCK!" I scream, coming hard on his face.

"That's a good girl," he praises me, watching my face.

I throw my arm across my face, spent. "I think I can get another one from you." He licks his lips, dragging his tongue over my clit. I jolt from being so sensitive. "Fuck me, Tristan." I reach down for him.

He kisses my clit one last time before he presses his mouth against mine, kissing me as he thrusts into me in one push. "GOD," I bite out, my eyes rolling back. It's like every single nerve ending is alive.

He lifts my thigh, burying himself even deeper inside of me. I can't even speak, breathe, all I can do is lie here and be at the mercy of Tristan.

"God, I could stay inside of you forever."

I clench down on him hard at his words. He reaches between us rubbing my clit sending me over the edge.

I bite his arm, trying not to wake the whole neighborhood. I'm done for this time, I don't have another one in me.

"You have killed me, it's official." I laugh, even my laugh sounds tired.

He chuckles, kissing my cheek. "I'll be back." He walks downstairs and I crawl off the bed, into the bathroom.

I look at myself in the mirror and I almost don't recognize myself with the happiness in my eyes. I touch my cheeks that are flushed, my hair is a mess but I have never felt more beautiful than I do in this moment. I use the bathroom, clean up and grab my hair brush off of the counter walking back into my bedroom.

Tristan has all of his clothes in his hands. "Uhh," I say confused, ignoring the fact we are both stark naked.

He finds a drawer and stuffs everything inside. "What are you doing?" I ask him.

He smirks, setting the bag into the closet. "Moving in," he says like it's the most normal thing.

I blink a few times coming to terms with what he is saying. "Wait, you're moving in?"

He nods. "I sure fucking am, no way am I leaving my girls."

My heart warms with him calling us his girls. "Well, why didn't you just say so?" I have a goofy smile on my face. I slide into bed and pull the blanket up to my chest covering myself.

"Let me." He sits down beside me, taking my hairbrush brushing through the strands getting out all of the knots.

I sit with my eyes closed, enjoying the moment. He brushes my hair over to one side, leaving the side of my neck bare. He presses a kiss there. "Beautiful and all mine." He grips my throat gently, tilting my head exactly the way he wanted it. "All yours," I confirm.

He starts to kiss my cheek when my phone goes off. I look at the clock on the nightstand and it reads two o' clock in the morning.

I pick up my phone and the caller ID says its Lani. "Hey is everything okay?" I ask immediately, putting the phone on speaker.

I hear sniffling in the background. "We have a sweet girl here who is homesick, she is wanting her mommy and Tristan," Lani says.

My heart breaks a little hearing her little cries in the background. Tristan is already out of the bed putting on his clothes and grabbing his keys.

"We will be right there, Lani," I tell her and hang up the phone, putting on a pair of leggings and a sweatshirt.

Tristan practically runs out of the house in his haste to get to her, it's way too cute honestly.

***

TRISTAN LITERALLY FLOORED it down the road to their house, it's hilarious. "Does she get homesick a lot?" he asks, his brow furrowed with worry.

"She has before," I tell him.

He slows down a little, turning to grin at me. "She asked for me too."

God, he's fucking precious. She has made his entire life without Michaela even knowing it.

Not going to lie, I love the fact that she asked for him too. She sees him as a part of her life and he brings her comfort. That's really important to me but especially Michaela.

We pull up in front of their house; Tristan practically jumps out of the truck, barely putting it into park before he comes around to help me out.

He takes my hand and I bite back a smile at his reaction. I

know he is trying to play it cool, but the thought of her needing him, I know it's killing him.

I knock on the door, both of us looking inside the glass door. I can hear them walking through the house to the door.

Trey comes around the corner holding Michaela in his arms, her head resting on her chest. She turns to look out of the window and her face changes from sad to happy in an instant.

Trey opens the door and Michaela reaches straight for Tristan. "Tristan!" she yells, wrapping her arms and legs around him like a monkey holding on.

He closes his eyes for a few seconds, taking in the moment of her hugging him. "Hi, baby girl. I heard you were sad." He rubs her back.

She nods. "I had a bad dream."

My heart hurts at her admission. "Thank you for taking such good care of her." I wrap my arm around Trey hugging him.

"I will babysit next so you guys can have a night out," I tell him.

He nods patting my shoulder. "I will sure take you up on that offer."

Tristan walks carrying Michaela. She's getting super big and before too long she'll be too big to carry, that breaks my heart because she's growing up on me.

I open the door for Tristan who sets Michaela in her seat, buckling her in. She yawns, closing her eyes.

"We will be home soon." He kisses her forehead so sweetly, shutting the door. All I can do is stare at him.

"What?" he asks, opening my door.

I climb inside and turn to him. "You love her, I can feel the way you love her," I admit to him.

He looks into the back seat. "She is mine," he admits to me, touching my face gently before shutting the door.

"You are ours too," I whisper into the truck.

10

LYNN

ONE WEEK LATER

WE PULL up in front of Walker's house. I try to calm the nerves in the pit of my stomach because we are spending the evening with Walker and Tristan's friend.

Walker has texted us every single day wanting us to bring Michaela over to him.

The second we pull up in front of his house, Walker walks out and straight to the back seat.

He opens the door and smiles at Michaela. "Hi sweetheart, I'm Walker, Tristan's dad." She takes him in, cautious at first before she relaxes. "Nice to meet you, kind sir," she says in that accent of hers and I stifle a laugh at his expression.

Tristan is flat out laughing. "Well, my lady can I help you out of the truck?" he asks her and I laugh at that getting out myself.

She nods. "That is much appreciated, sir."

He lifts her out of the truck and smiles down at her then turns to look at me. "It's nice to see you again, Lynn."

I walk over and give him a side hug. "It's nice to see you too."

"So princess, I do have a surprise for you," he tells Michaela who jumps up and down. "Oh my God! What is it?

"Let me show you." He leads her behind the house and we

109

follow and as we turn the corner, I see a huge playhouse that looks like a mini castle.

Michaela doesn't say a word, she just points and looks at the castle and then to Walker. "Do you like it?" he inquires.

"I LOVE IT!" she screams, shaking from the excitement.

He chuckles as she drags him to the playhouse, opening the door. I follow behind him, really touched that he did this for her. "Your dad is really great," I tell Tristan.

He nods. "My dad has always been such a great dad; he did stuff like this for me all of the time growing up. One of his biggest regrets is that he didn't know about Joslyn until she was already grown."

I remember hearing about that, they found out she was his daughter by an unlikely chance.

"I hope they have a good relationship now." I can't imagine not knowing Michaela and then finding out when she was much older in life.

He nods. "They do, ever since he found out he made it his mission to be a part of her life."

I can see them in the window, she's holding a doll and putting a crown on Walker's head. He's sitting on an itty-bitty chair made for a kid.

Tristan laughs and pulls me inside of the playhouse with them, I'm in awe. He has really gone all out with the decorations, it even has air conditioning. "Wow, this is absolutely beautiful," I tell Walker.

He doesn't take his eyes off Michaela who is slipping on a princess dress over her clothes, and plopping a crown on her head. "You look beautiful," Walker tells her.

She flashes her smile, which is so adorable because she's missing teeth in the front.

She sits down in the chair next to him and looks around the room. "Thank you, Walker. I really love it." She leans over and hugs him.

He closes his eyes, holding her back tightly. "You are welcome, baby girl."

She sits back holding her doll, brushing its hair. "So, I guess that means you are my grandpa, I have always wanted one of those."

I almost have a heart attack on the spot. Walker smirks at me seeing my expression. "I would love to be your grandpa."

She giggles. "Well I mean mom and Tristan are boyfriend, girlfriend, so I guess that makes him my dad," she says so simply.

Someone could push me over with a feather; she doesn't understand the magnitude of her words.

I am sure it's a confusing thing for her. I have never dated anyone in my life until Tristan and have never had any man in her life but those she is related to and the ones in the club she considers her uncles.

I slip out of the playhouse needing air and I need to speak to Tristan about all of this because I'm so confused. I march across the grass to the small pond so I can look at the fish, a hand slips in mine stopping me.

He turns me around. "Tell me your thoughts right now," he demands of me. I can tell that he's concerned.

I let out a deep breath, trying to catch up with my thoughts and feelings right now.

"She loves you Tristan, she really does. She is starting to see you as a father figure and that worries me because what if you don't want to be?"

We have never talked about this before. We have been going with the flow the last month and I never dreamed that she would get so attached to him so fast.

She really loves him; she comes to him for comfort like she does me.

I can see the pain in his eyes because I'm doubting him, sometimes I just need the words. "Baby, I am not ever going to leave you. I would adopt Michaela right now if I could because I love her, but I also love her mom with everything in me."

I couldn't stop the tears if I wanted to. "I love you too, Tristan." I mean every single word.

He pulls me to him, his lips slamming against mine. He kisses me so thoroughly, like he's trying to engrain in me to never doubt him again.

He is everything I never allowed myself to wish for, I know it's crazy and it happened all so fast.

When you meet your person, you just know, every rule is thrown out of the window.

Time around us stands still, locked in this moment together.

God, I do love him.

I've loved him since the second he held me and Michaela all night long after her nightmares; when he slept on the floor next to us to make sure we were okay.

Since the second he came into our life, he has taken care of us in every way. But even more, he showed me what it's like to be truly loved by someone.

"Woohoo!" Michaela yells and I break the kiss, slightly dizzy. She's smiling at us, clapping and Walker is leaning against the playhouse. Darren walks over to join Walker clapping himself.

"Come on in, let's eat dinner." Walker waves everyone inside into the dining room where the food is set up, my eyes zeroing in on the barbecue wings.

"Who cooked this?" Tristan asks, holding my seat out for me to sit and Michaela sits in front of us between Walker and Darren.

Walker chuckles. "I wish I could cook like this but I got it catered."

Tristan laughs. "I was wondering because this looks too good to be your cooking." He takes a bite of the ribs.

Walker glares at him, Tristan keeps on grinning completely unfazed. I am not sure if Tristan knows but his dad is scary.

"Aww papa bear has a grumpy face." Michaela reaches up to his cheeks pushing his face up in a smile. "See, much better."

His face softens. "Thank you baby, you helped me."

She looks so proud. "Well thanks, kind sir." She pats his massive forearm and goes back to her food.

Walker looks at Michaela like the world ends and begins with her just like my Tristan.

I want my baby to have all of the people in her life, she deserves to be loved and to have a huge support base.

Tristan puts his hand under the table, stuffing it between my legs holding onto my thigh tightly. I try to play it cool but that touch alone has something throbbing. Tristan has woken something up in me.

I lick my lips, opening my legs a little giving him better access. His head swings in my direction, shocked I'd done that.

"Oh Lynn, want to see my old bedroom?" Tristan asks suddenly, standing up. Everyone looks at him confused.

I school my features. "Sure, I would love to."

I avoid looking at Walker and Darren not wanting to give anything away. Tristan practically drags me out of the dining room upstairs to his bedroom.

I giggle trying to keep up with him. He pushes open the door and locks it behind him.

"Someone has been a naughty little girl." He takes my hand pressing it against him, letting me feel what I have done to him.

I tighten my hand on him. "Baby, I can't just help myself. Want to see what you have done to me?" I'm being bold.

I pull down my pants, climb onto the bed, bending over to show him how soaked my underwear is.

He bites his lip, his eyes hooded. "Fuck me, what a sight you are."

His hands grab my hips, kissing the small of my back, little by little moving down to my ass cheeks, biting.

I feel his warm breath against me, I bite the bedspread not

wanting to be loud.He bites my panties, slightly nipping my clit and I almost fall down. "Mmm, I think I could have you for every single meal."

My legs are shaking as I struggle to be still and not force him to touch me. He grips my panties on the side, tearing them off my body.

"Hey." I start to argue but the feel of his tongue moving through my folds shuts me up.

"God, you are the best thing I have ever tasted. I can never get enough of you," he says in between licks.

I'm out of my mind with pleasure, all I can do is focus on what he is doing to me.

He stops suddenly and I turn around just as he slides inside me. I close my eyes at the feeling of being filled.

"I will never grow tired of you inside me," I moan, arching my back bringing him in deeper.

He throws his head back, eyes closed, soaking in the moment just like I am. There is nothing better than seeing someone you care about fall apart because of you.

He pulls all the way out, just leaving the tip before slamming back in, hard. I bite my hand so I don't make any noise, my eyes rolling back into my head.

"I am yours to do whatever you want to."

I know what my words do to him, his hand on my hip tightens. "That's such a good girl," he whispers in my ear, rubbing my ass cheek as he praises me.

I keep my arms in front of me, shutting out everything and just feel. The way that he moves, the way that he knows exactly how to drive me crazy.

I clench down onto him so hard, loving the way that he can make me fall apart. "I am so close."

"I can feel it." He moves faster, his fingers rubbing my clit. I clench my eyes shut, my legs giving out as I come harder than I ever have before.

I twist the blanket under me, my legs now in between Tristan's as he moves inside of me faster, harder, as he chases his orgasm.

"I want one more from you."

He presses his fingers against my ass, pushing but not entering. I can't even breathe as I chase it.

"FUCK," I whisper over and over into the bed as I come hard once more and Tristan follows me, filling me. "Such a good girl." I clench down hard on him at his words.

He chokes, that's what he gets.

He slips out of me, leaving me face-down onto the bed and I hear him in the bathroom turning the water on.

He comes back turning me over, cleaning me. "I do love you," I tell him.

He leans over me, kissing me. "I really love you too."

I smile wrapping my arms around him, just holding him. "We better get back before they wonder."

Tristan chuckles. "Baby, they are not wondering. They know what we are doing up here."

I cover my face. "Please don't tell me that."

He kisses my cheek laughing. "Your red cheeks are so adorable, your face is cute too."

I smack him on the arm gently, "Ha ha." I pretend to laugh.

I climb off the bed and I look down at my demolished panties. Tristan scoops them up and puts them in his pocket. "I will keep these with me."

I roll my eyes, putting my leggings on without my underwear. I walk to the mirror and attempt to fix my hair.

"You look so beautiful."

I smile at him in the mirror as he watches me. "You just like that you made me look this way."

He shrugs his shoulder, grinning. "I do love when you look freshly fucked."

I turn around kissing him once more, taking his hand. "Let's go and finish our dinner."

"I already ate, baby," he jokes.

The second we walk into the dining room, Walker and Darren both stare at us, eyebrows arched.

I decide to play it cool and sit down at the table eating my food. Michaela is eating ice cream.

"Does Tristan got games in his room?" Michaela asks.

I instantly start to sweat, horrified. "What do you mean, baby?" I ask.

She shrugs. "You were gone a long time, so I was wondering if you were playing a game."

Please just end me now, put me out of my misery. Tristan is holding his face, laughing. Darren looks like he is going to pass out and Walker doesn't even care, he is holding his stomach letting it all out.

I'm so glad they are enjoying my embarrassment.

"Do you like your ice cream?" I change the subject.

She nods. "Yes, it's got little cookies in it!" She lifts her bowl for me to see.

I glare at all three of the guys, which just sets them off once again. I eat my food, not speaking to any of them.

"Can you play dolls with me?" Michaela asks and takes Walker and Darren's hands leading them out of the room because they were done eating.

I can feel Tristan staring at me, but I ignore him. He moves so he face is in front of me but I look down at my plate pretending to be mad. "Be a good girl and look at me."

Fuck.

I look up and he smiles, reaching forward touching my face. "You are so beautiful, it fucking hurts me sometimes."

All of the mock anger is gone, leaving just the feeling of love. I lean over and rest my head against his chest snuggling.

His hand rubs down my back and then back up through my hair and scalp. "I will fall asleep if you don't stop."

"Take a nap honey, you need it from working all day long." He leads me to the couch and covers me with a blanket. "I will go outside with them, rest good, baby." He kisses me on my forehead.

I watch him through the window slipping inside of the play-house with Walker and Darren.

They're so cute.

I tuck the blanket under my chin, closing my eyes feeling so content and happy.

Lynn

I WAKE up to someone running their hands down my arm, I know who it is instantly. I smile opening my eyes, coming face to face with Tristan's stomach. Tristan is holding my head in his lap. "You had a great nap, sweetheart." He bends over kissing me on the cheek.

I hear my baby's sweet giggles. I look over to see her sitting on the floor with Walker, who has a princess tiara on his head and playing dolls with her.

"So, I heard from a birdie that you love Halloween and tonight is an open night of a haunted trail. Do you want to go?" Tristan asks me, tucking my hair behind my ear.

I sit up. "Uhh I would love to go!" I get so excited, I haven't been to one in years and I have been dying to go.

"Let me call my friend Summer to see if she wants to go." My friend is also the therapist who Michaela sees.

"Oh, wait. Who is going to watch Michaela?" I ask Tristan.

"Etta already agreed." He lets me know that he has this fully planned.

"Alright then." I kiss his cheek, sitting up so I can text Summer to see if she is wanting to go.

"Walker, Darren you just have to come with us," I tell them.

"We sure will," Walker tells me and Darren nods.

I would sell my left tit if they would get scared, I do know Summer is a huge chicken.

She texts me back almost instantly. "I'm so down. Want me to drive to your house?"

"Summer wants to know if she should drive to my house?" I ask Tristan.

Tristan shakes his head no. "We will come get her. She doesn't need to be out driving this late."

There goes my heart once again, he is such a gentleman. "We'll drive to your house," I text her back. Walker offers then takes a fake sip of a small little plastic teacup as Michaela feeds her baby.

My poor heart, I'm not sure I can take the cuteness.

"Let's get going then, it's going to get dark soon." Tristan stands, taking me with him.

Michaela puts her doll down onto the floor next to Walker. "Thank you for letting me play with it."

He lifts the doll tucking it back in her arm. "It's yours, sweetheart, take it home with you," he smiles.

She jumps on him giving him a huge squeeze. "I think I will get you dolls everyday if you give me hugs like this," he jokes to her.

She giggles, "You're a silly papa bear." She takes ahold of his ears, tugging on them.

"Are you making fun of my ears, princess?" He mock growls at her, then lifts her up in the air and catches her.

"That was fun!" she squeals and tugs on his ears once again so he will do it again.

Walker throws her to Darren and I notice Tristan keeps raising his arms like he is wanting to snatch her away.

"Fuck, don't drop her," he stresses and snatches her from Darren.

I laugh loudly at him being overprotective, he sets her on the ground and takes her hand. "Ready to spend the evening with Etta? We will come get you before bed," he tells her, squeezing her little hand.

It has literally stressed him out that she was so homesick, even though he was thrilled that she asked for him. So, it was a win/lose for him.

"Okay, can you read me a story tonight?" she asks him as they walk to the door together. "Sure can, think on what you want me to read." They walk out of the door and I just watch them leave taking in the moment.

I look at Walker. "You have raised the best son," I tell him honestly, because he did.

Walker walks to me, patting me on the back. "I taught him to take care of those he loves, because if he didn't, I would beat his ass." I roll my eyes at such a guy response.

"See you guys in a bit!" I call over my shoulder wanting to catch up to Tristan and Michaela.

11

LYNN

"I am so excited!" I rub my hands together; this is my favorite time of the year. I take Halloween seriously. I'm in a competition with the ladies at the club to see who brings the best candy.

I'm the champion of course because I use Michaela to tell me what the kids are jiving with.

"Have you ever thought about what if a crazy person shows up to one of these pretending to a part of the haunt and they're really crazy?"

Tristan looks at me in horror. "Fuck no! But now that is all I am going to think about."

I laugh. "Ahh, you're a badass SEAL. I am sure they won't even try to scare us in fear of you guys."

Tristan shoots me a pleased grin because I stroked his ego. We pull up in front of a cute little white house. I reach over and honk the horn letting Summer know we are here.

"Walker, have you ever been to a haunted trail before?" I ask him.

But he doesn't even acknowledge me, doesn't even look at me. He is busy looking at something over my shoulder and so is Darren.

"Hey, you okay?" I ask Darren who looks like he literally might have a heart attack.

But he doesn't answer me either. What the heck?

I turn around to see what they are looking at and Summer is walking down her driveway to the truck.

I guess I should have mentioned that she is absolutely beautiful, but her heart? She is the kindest woman I have ever met.

Walker opens the truck door coming to his senses the fastest, stepping out smiling at her. The most beautiful thing is, it reaches his eyes.

I give Tristan a side-eyed glance wondering if he is witnessing the same thing I am. Darren is still silent, watching her every move.

"Let me help you inside, darlin'," he tells her, taking her hand and helping her inside of the truck.

She scoots to the middle, in between the both of them. They are both massive guys, so she is squished in between the both of them.

Darren has literally not stopped staring at her. Summer's face is growing redder by the second. She looks at her lap, trying to play it cool.

But I know she is dying on the inside. She is just as much as a man reject as me.

She had a really amazing childhood, unlike me, but she is really shy and purehearted. A lot of men have tried to take advantage of that. She sensed that growing up, so she threw herself into her work and helping others.

Her heart is so beautiful.

Tristan gives me a secret grin, putting the truck into reverse. "Summer, how was work today?" I ask her.

She smiles at me. "It was hard. I had a few more trauma cases. Those are always hard."

I nod my head in agreement. No matter how much you try

to close off your emotions to it, it bothers you, especially since I deal with a lot of girls recovering from being in the cult.

"I am going to the veterans center next week. I'm going to see some soldiers who are experiencing severe PTSD." Her face falls. One of the reasons why she became a therapist was because one of her dads used to be in the military and PTSD wrecked his life for a bit.

Darren looks at her with such respect. "Tristan and Darren just got out of the SEAL a month or so ago," I tell her, giving Darren some perks, nodding to Darren.

She looks at him, her face glowing. "Wow! Thank you both for your service."

Tristan looks in the mirror at his dad. "Walker was in the special forces until I was born."

She looks from Darren to Walker. I know she thinks both of them are attractive because I can see it written all over her face. "My dads were special forces but Knox, one of my dads, was kidnapped, held captive for days. He was haunted by that for years."

Walker bursts out laughing suddenly. "Fuck, I knew your dads! I was in the forces with them."

Well, isn't this a small world.

Summer grins. "That's amazing! I am sure they would love to know that I met you tonight."

Walker gives Darren a look, one that I can't decipher.

Okay, weirdos.

Soon we are pulling up to the haunted trail. I see a small line of people facing the woods with someone with a flashlight at the entrance.

Tristan walks over to my door, opening it for me and taking ahold of my hand which, I am grateful for because I hear a ton of girls screaming deep into the woods. Chills run down my spine, one because of fear and the other with anticipation. "Oh my God," Summer whispers when she hears the chainsaw.

I laugh when I see a clown chasing someone out of the woods, the person falls which reminds me of all too much of a scary movie.

Tristan tucks me closer when someone runs past us to cut in line in front of us, almost running into us.

Then two more guys run past us to join the other guy. I roll my eyes at the ridiculousness when they start yelling and pushing on each other.

Tristan leads us to the ticket booth and before I can even argue Walker walks straight in front of all us, handing a hundred-dollar bill to the worker.

"What the fuck, Dad?"

Walker turns around giving Tristan a look. "Tristan," he says gruffly in a dad voice, then turns back to the worker, taking our wristbands.

I cover my mouth so I don't laugh at Walker's gruffness. Tristan just shakes his head smiling not taking his dad serious.

I know Walker is a softy, because a little girl named Michaela brought that out in full force with the tiara on his head.

We all get in line, right behind the super rowdy guys. I turn around to Summer, who is eyeing the woods like they are going to come out any second and snatch her.

"Have you ever been to one of these before?" I ask her.

She shakes her head no. "I was a chicken when I was younger." Not even looking at me, she just eyes the woods.

"When you were younger?" I question.

She looks at me, eyes squinted together. "What were you saying?"

I bite my lips together. "Nothing." I shrug.

She laughs and wraps her arm through mine. "Just don't let me get taken by a scary man and I will be fine."

Darren steps to her. "You're safe with me." He winks at her.

She turns away hiding her smile. "Thank you, Darren."

I arch an eyebrow at him, then look at Summer. He shrugs. "I

123

would protect you with my life, darlin." Walker steps up to her, putting himself in front of her so she is looking at him.

Wait, are both of them interested in her?

Well, hmm.

The guys in front of us go through the line, getting on the hayride that leads to the beginning of the trail.

The lady at the entrance looks at our wristbands, then we step inside through the gate waiting for our ride.

The lights pop up over the trees letting us know that they are coming. "Oh gosh, I am nervous," I whisper to Tristan, scooting a little closer to him.

He wraps his arm around me, rubbing my arm to make sure I am warm. The ride pulls to a stop. "GET ON," a man with a very evil sounding voice says causing me to jump.

Tristan walks in front of me, I grab the back of his shirt huddling in close. He steps up, taking my hand helping me inside then Summer. Walker sits on the edge of the ride, on the other side of Summer.

The ride takes off. I look onto the foggy road to see if I can see someone up ahead.

The guys are way too calm; Summer and I on the other hand look like we are going to hyperventilate.

I was way too cool with this idea until we got on the ride.

All of a sudden, a chainsaw starts out of nowhere. I duck my head when someone jumps onto the hayride with us waving the chainsaw.

Summer screams holding her face and I hunch down into Tristan's lap who is laughing.

I peek up under my hands to see freaking Michael Myers in my face.

They jump off of the hayride and I look at Summer. "I will never make fun of you again." She laughs at me, both of us acted like total loons.

Maybe after this we will be used to it and it won't be so bad.

She grips my hand hard and I hold onto Tristan. I am ready to wrench her over to me in case someone does that again.

The hayride stops and Jeepers Creepers comes out of a barn with an axe. He shows his nasty grin. Oh my God.

He throws something at us, I watch as it lands in Summer's lap. My eyes widen when I see it's an eyeball. He points at Summer then curls his finger in a come-hither motion.

Oh hell no.

She just got singled out.

She grips my hand so hard. "Maybe we should just head back?" she suggests.

"GET OFF THE RIDE." The guy driving the hayride is looking around at us, his face half melted off.

Walker steps off the ride first and we all follow; Summer is holding onto my hand for dear life. The Jeepers Creepers guy is slowly walking over to us. I look down at the ground not wanting to make eye contact.

I feel hot, nasty smelling breath on my face. He is blowing so hard, my hair moves with every breath. I step back away from the person, back into Tristan. The guy steps in between me and Summer, separating us.

"Uhh," I say out loud and try to scoot around him but he blocks my path moving until he is chest to chest with me pretty much and then rubs his chest against my boobs. Tristan starts to pull me back but he grips my upper arms hard and screams at the top of his lungs in my face.

"What the fuck?" Tristan growls, pushing him out of my face and he hits the ground hard. He turns around and looks behind him at Summer and the guys. His face changes to one of pure rage. Weirdo.

I take my cue to run to catch up with Summer pulling Tristan with me, who keeps looking back at the guy.

Summer is holding onto the back of Walker's shirt like he is her lifeline, she turns around to look at me. "What the fuck was his problem?!" she asks me, taking ahold of my hand, noticing him still staring at her.

Tristan has both of his hands on my hips which is making me feel better. I peek back and see the Jeepers Creepers guy running through the woods further up the trail away from us.

As long as I don't have to see him again. "I think that fucker has small penis syndrome," I mutter under my breath, feeling creeped out that he screamed in my face like that.

Summer snorts and then I burst out laughing with her, the laughter is the medicine I needed.

I see a little torch hanging off of the tree, giving us some light. Just as we pass the tree a man jumps out holding the torch and Summer screams, and I laugh.

We make it to a small little haunted house, walking up the steps. A small window slides up and a huge ass arm flops out at our heads then freaking Santa Claus pops his head out of the little hole. He says, "Come on, children," then flops the arm again.

"What the fuck?" Darren laughs at the evil Santa and stops when he sees someone sitting in the chair.

I peek around Walker's arm to see if it's a real person but it looks like a dummy to me. Darren steps closer, putting his face next to his then all of a sudden the dummy comes to life scaring the piss out of him.

Tristan almost falls to the ground laughing at Darren, Darren is on the ground on his butt. "Are you hurt?" Summer takes his hand and tries to help him up.

He smiles at her. "I'm fine, darlin." He stands up but he doesn't let go of her hand.

Walker leads us through the house with me and Tristan bringing up the rear. A little child comes out from under the table scaring the piss out of me.

"Oh my God! Are you missing your parents?" I ask her,

concerned why a little kid would be here and by herself in the back room.

She hisses at me like a cat and sneaks back under the table. "Well I guess she works here."

We step outside of the house and a chainsaw starts up, banging against the wall of the fence.

Tristan wraps his arm around me. I eye the chainsaw man as he runs straight toward us then I watch in horror as he trips over a tree root and falls straight on his face on top of the chainsaw.

Oh my God.

"Are you okay?" I ask him, walking over to him.

He nods and pushes himself up to a sitting position. I start to help him when I hear grown men screaming at the top of their lungs.

The guy on the ground looks so confused. "The trail ended here with me," he says, pushing himself up to a standing position.

Tristan takes my hand and pulls me to him as the guy carries his chainsaw and walks up the trail to around the corner.

Then he starts screaming, a bloodcurdling scream.

What the fuck?

I look at Tristan scared out of my mind.

Just as I am about to speak one of the weird guys from the beginning of the trail is running straight toward us and he is missing his arm. It's not a fake missing arm but literally blood dripping down his arm.

"Oh my God!" Summer whispers over and over under her breath.

He falls to the ground in front of us, his eyes wide, his face pale. "Run," he tells us and faceplants onto the ground.

We are staring down at him in horror. I am ready for someone to pop out of the woods and be like you've been punk'd.

A chainsaw starts up and I can hear the sounds of something being cut up. "Fuck we need to get through the woods."

Tristan literally carries me into the woods away from the trail and Darren is carrying Summer. We make it about thirty feet into the woods when I see the fucking Jeepers Creepers guy with a machete in one hand as he tosses a chainsaw onto the ground with the other.

He looks around the ground seeing the guy with his arm cut off and smiles that weird fucking smile.

"Oh my God, Tristan! The little girl." My heart sinks at the idea of her getting hurt.

The Jeepers Creepers guy turns to look into the woods where we are standing. Fuck, I think he heard me.

"Jeepers Creepers, where did you get those peepers?" he starts to sing and I think I might pass out.

This is my worst fear. "I jinxed us," I whisper in horror, it's all my fault.

Tristan puts his hand around my mouth to stop me from talking as the guy takes a step in our direction in the woods.

"Ohh Summer!" he states randomly in a calming tone.

She looks completely pale. "We need to fucking go, now. I know him," she whisper yells to us.

Walker takes her hand and we all take off at a sprint in the woods towards the lights at the main entrance.

I can hear the guy running behind us, this is literally my worst nightmare. Tristan pulls me in front of him as I start lagging behind because I keep on looking back.

We reach the field which leaves us right in the open.

"Mommy, where are you?" I hear a small child ask.

I stop dead in my tracks and I see the little girl from the haunted house walking out of the woods into the field just as the Jeepers Creepers guy does.

She looks at him. "Josh, have you seen my mommy?" she asks

him then she looks at us, then back at the guy who I am assuming is Josh.

He looks at Summer grinning. "I have waited so long to get revenge." He points his machete at her.

He takes off his mask and I am completely shocked when I see who it is, we have a right to be fucking scared.

He is a serial killer that Summer put away.

"Josh, what are you doing?" the little girl asks, moving closer to him.

He looks at her and smiles a crazy smile, causing my heart to sink. "Your mommy is dead sweetheart, want to see her?" He reaches into his pocket pulling a piece of skin that still has hair attached to it.

He fucking scalped her.

"Joshua, you don't need to do this," Summer tells him.

He glares at her. "I do need to do this! You put me away!" he screams as the spit flies from his mouth. We can all hear the police sirens in the distance behind us.

He points the machete once more at Summer. "I will be back for you, bitch." He throws it at her then takes off running deeper into the woods.

Walker picks her up, turning her around away from the machete so it moves past her by just mere inches.

"What the fuck?" Darren takes off after him, following him into the darkness.

"Fuck," Tristan growls. "Dad, take the girls to the truck; I am going after him." Tristan pulls his gun out of the back of his pants.

I can hear bullets going off in the distance, the little girl starts crying. "Come here, sweetheart." I wave her over and she runs to me.

Walker picks her up and we all take off running to the truck which is the first safe place we see. He helps all of us inside and makes sure we lock the doors before he takes off running to where the guys just were.

Random police pop out of everywhere with guns. I can hear bullets going off all around us.

Then we see nothing, everyone is buried deep into the woods. Our eyes search through the trees to see if we see anyone.

We can hear the screams, the sounds of bullets going off. Then silence, minutes pass that feel like hours.

I cover my mouth with my hand, watching as bodies on top of bodies are being carried out of the woods.

Some are screaming holding onto various wounds on their body, some are slumped over.

Vomit crawls up my throat. How many people did he kill? How many did he hurt?

I take my eyes off the traumatic scene to turn and check on the little girl. She is lying on the back seat crying at the top of her lungs. I can't imagine how scared she was. "Sweetheart, was your mom working here?" I ask her.

I pray that her mom wasn't actually hurt and that he was lying to just scare her. "She worked in the ticket booth."

I put my face up to the window to see if I can see out and I see a lady who was in the ticket booth running around holding the top of her head. "Is that your mom?" I ask her, pointing.

"MOMMY," she screams.

I roll down the window and I yell for her, her daughter in my lap yelling too. She turns to look at us and she falls to the ground with relief when she sees her daughter.

She manages to stand and starts toward us when a man dressed as Michael is carrying a knife running straight toward her.

Oh my God, no.

There can't be more than one?

"He is not a part of the haunt," the little girl whispers.

Her mom takes off running. I push open the door holding it open for her and she manages to jump inside just before he reaches her.

"Get back!" I scream, slamming the door shut and locking it.

He stabs the glass with his knife, over and over again, trying to get inside but the glass doesn't budge.

They crawl into the back seat and Summer crawls up front with me. "If he wants to fucking play, let's play." Getting pissed off, my momma bear instincts are kicking into high gear. My aggression only escalates as the little girl continues to cry, seeing all of the blood pouring from her mom's head where he scalped a portion of it.

Summer takes off her jacket, handing it to her so she can put pressure on the wound. I put the truck into reverse and back up away from the fake fucking Michael Myers.

He looks at us, waving his knife.

"I hope he likes the taste of rubber," I tell Summer, grinning.

She holds onto the dashboard as I floor it right toward him. He tries to take off running but he doesn't make it far. His head hits the top of truck, then he's pulled under it.

Bounce

Bounce

Bounce

We are all silent as we look out of the window to see him lying on the ground but much to my shock he is trying to stand up.

"What the fuck? Is he superhuman?" I ponder.

"Well, I guess I will just have to put it in reverse." I put the truck in reverse and back up until I feel the bounce again. This time I don't bother driving completely away from him and keep the truck's front tires on his body.

I see the guys coming out of the window, all three of them. They look like they just went to war.

They see the truck and take off toward to us. Tristan opens

the door and looks at all of us. "He got away but I saw some other crazy fuckers in the woods, we tied them up for the police."

We hear a moan from under the truck, Tristan bends over and looks under the truck. I slide out and I take in the damage. He is lying under there, his leg against the tire at a very funny angle.

Chaos is happening all around us, screams of women and men who are injured. Police running into the woods.

"Why is there a guy under your truck, Tristan?" Darren asks, looking under it with Tristan.

"Well, he came after us with a knife," I tell them, pointing to the window where it's scratched.

"Well fuck, you should have run over his head," Walker growls quickly, getting into the truck moving off of the guy under the truck.

Tristan reaches under the truck, grabbing him by his hair. He is beyond pissed. He literally drags him, making sure to hit every rock, his face on the ground getting skinned to bits.

He throws him down to a police officer's feet, pointing to us and then down at him. My guess explaining what happened.

I open the back door, checking on the woman who is hurt. "Can I take you to the hospital?" I ask her concerned.

She nods. Lifting the jacket off her head I try not to make a face at how horrible it looks. I can literally see her skull. "What happened?" I ask her, helping her fix the shirt.

"Josh went literally crazy. I began to ask him what happened when all of a sudden, he reaches inside the ticket booth, pulls me out by my hair and starts dragging me into the woods. He kept on calling me Summer over and over and mumbling weird things. One of the guys who worked here tried to get me loose, but he wouldn't let go. So, he used his knife to cut me loose but he got my scalp too."

What the fuck?

I really look at her and it hits me that she looks exactly like Summer. Like they could almost be twins.

Summer is horrified and she covers her face. I know she is blaming herself.

"Wanda!" a man screams, running through the parking lot. "Frank!" she yells and the man runs over to her. "Daddy," the little girl sobs and jumps to him. Frank almost falls to the ground at the sight of his wife.

I step back letting him take them out of the truck. "Thank you for taking care of them," he expresses, taking his family with him.

Tristan returns and he pulls me to his chest. I bury my face deep, completely shocked and heartbroken for Summer and all of these other people who suffered tonight.

I hear her let out a sob and I turn to hug her but I see her right in between Walker and Darren both of them hugging her.

My heart hurts seeing her like this. "It's not your fault, Summer. You did the right thing all those years ago."

She nods against Walker's chest, Darren is rubbing her back. Walker looks like he is willing to burn down the whole world and Darren looks like he is going to help him.

"Let's go home. Stay with us tonight okay, Summer?" I beg of her. Tristan kisses the top of my head. I can feel him shaking, I know it's from anger.

I never expected this to happen.

"Who is Josh?" Tristan asks.

Summer lets out a deep breath. "He used to be my best friend, we grew up together. He lived next door, stayed all night with me."

"Until I noticed that the animals in town started being murdered, we would find more every single day. The way they died grew even worse." She wipes under her eyes.

"My dads were on hyperalert and we had Josh stay with us because his home life was bad. His behavior started to change at school, he would poke people with needles in school; he would literally do people harm for no reason."

She moves until she is sitting in the truck facing us. "But he played it off as a joke. Then I grew uncomfortable with him so I told my dads. They wouldn't let him stay anymore."

She looks at us haunted. "He went crazy," she whispers. "We would find eyeballs on our front porch, under my outside window. We didn't know it was Josh at the time until I caught him murdering an animal in the back yard."

I am sick to my stomach even though I have heard this before. "I told my dads and they called the police. But when they got to his house, he was gone."

"He broke into our house in the middle of the night. My dads found him standing above me with a knife over his head ready to kill me. My dad tackled him and tied him up until the police took him away."

"That's when we found out girls in town were murdered and it was him, all the girls looked just like me. He was fifteen at the time. I thought he was still in jail; I think him finding me here was just a crazy thing."

She covers her face. "I need to call my dads." She takes out her phone but Walker takes it from her. "I will call them myself. Let's get you to Lynn's and we can figure all of this shit out. We need to tell all of the guys; we need to protect the women."

Lynn

TRISTAN and I are tucking Michaela into her bed with Tristan reading to her about a little girl discovering that she was a princess.

Tristan couldn't get to Michaela fast enough after all that

happened tonight and I am not going to lie, I needed to be with her too.

Seeing that little girl and what happened all around her? It made me realize life is so fragile. My heart is breaking for Summer; what happened to her as a teenager has been very hard on her.

"Mommy, why is Summer so sad?" Michaela asks me, bringing me out of my thoughts.

I take her little hand in mine. "Sweet girl, sometimes people just get really sad and it's okay," I reassure her.

She looks at Tristan. "I get sad sometimes too, but then I think of fun things and I feel better."

Tristan smiles at her, that special look on his face that is reserved just for her. "If you are ever sad, you come to me and your mommy, okay?" He smooths her hair out of her face.

"I love you guys," she whispers, her little eyes opening slower each time.

Tristan looks at me like she just shot him straight in the heart. I scoot up the bed lying on one side of her as Tristan lays on her other side.

I take his hand as we both stare into her sleeping face. "We love you so much, sweetheart." I kiss her forehead.

The love you have for your child is unlike anything you will ever feel in your life, it's all-consuming.

Tristan squeezes my hand. "I love you both."

My heart squeezes, I can't believe that this is actually my life. I never dreamed that I would be this happy.

We both lay with her, staring into her precious little face until she is deep into sleep.

Tristan helps me out of her bed so I don't wake her up. We pull her door shut and make our way downstairs to check on Walker, Darren, and Summer.

"Are you guys hungry?" I ask, turning the corner but stop dead in my tracks shushing Tristan as both take in the scene.

Summer is fast asleep with her head in Walker's lap, Darren is tucked in behind her holding her tightly.

Walker is staring at us. "There is a guest room right through there if you want." I whisper to Walker not to wake her.

He nods, gently nudging Darren awake and scoops Summer up in his arms, walking into guest room with Darren right behind him, shutting the door.

"Well, I never expected this shit," Tristan says in the silence staring at the door they just closed.

I laugh. "Honey me either, but I want happiness for everyone. All of them deserve it and if they find it in each other, I'm happy."

12

LYNN

TWO MONTHS LATER

WE ALL RUN off the party bus laughing. We're having a girls' night and everyone decided that it's time to prank people's yards.

The first stops are cult members who will get all of the shit they deserve. I have a bag of forks, pressing them into the ground with Adeline helping me. We are laughing so hard, for really no reason and we can barely stand up.

Shaylin opens the truck throwing glitter inside everywhere that will never come out of the truck. Jean is busy with a baseball bat taking out the mailbox, she was drunk before she even got on the bus. She just leaned against the window, laughing and snorting.

The light comes on inside the house, we all scream and take off running to the bus. Alisha falls face-first; we all reach down and pick her up practically dragging her with us.

We pack onto the bus, our faces smashed against the window watching as they walk out of their house holding their face in disbelief at the sight of their home. The prospect takes off like lightning away from the crime scene.

I don't feel an ounce of guilt because every one of these

people we are making miserable has destroyed others in one way or another.

"Next house!" Jean screams at the top of her lungs and we all laugh at her antics. The next house is literally right down the road.

Etta is the first one off the bus, throwing toilet paper over the house. Joslyn has a box of nails throwing it under their vehicle. Gracelyn is painting nasty words on the side of their house, which is hilarious to me since she is the softest one out of us all but Summer may give her a run for her money.

The light turns on and I run to the bus with a few girls while Etta, Gracelyn, and Paisley hide behind the bush.

We all peek out of the window so we can watch their reaction, Jean is lying face-down into one of the seats.

I smile when I hear the man yell, "What the fuck is this?"

Weird, his voice is really familiar. I move closer to the window, holding my hand up to the glass to block the glare so I can see better.

Then a woman comes out of the house gasping dramatically. "Oh my God, who did this?"

I take a few steps back, my heart pounding so hard in my chest at the realization of who it is.

I look at Shaylin, who is shaking me and asking me what is happening but I don't answer. I can only stare at my mother and Etta's ex-husband, Michael.

My mother kisses him on his cheek, running her hand down his chest like she is trying to soothe him.

My head is shaking side to side, I'm in such shock and disbelief at what I'm seeing. Oh my God, Etta.

I had it rough but Etta had it worse than I did; Michael hated her and my mother hated Etta. They were so mean to her; my mother knew of how horrible Michael treated Etta but she would laugh it off and told her to take it. Could this be the reason?

My husband was horrible to me too, but it doesn't touch what Etta went through and that forever breaks my heart.

The second the door shuts, Etta and the girls run over to the bus; I stand waiting for her. I need to hold her and make sure she is okay. This is so bad.

It's not because they are together; it's the betrayal of our already shitty mother. We always had hoped that she would be better for us but it never happened. She is so much worse than we could have ever dreamt.

"Etta, I can't believe it," I gasp.

Etta doesn't even speak, she sits down in the seat looking like she is on the brink of a major panic attack.

I move to her, taking her hands bending down in front of her. "That part of your life is over Etta, don't let them have the satisfaction of fucking with you," I tell her.

"What the fuck is happening?" Shaylin asks us.

I look at Shaylin, anger burning so deep inside of me. "That was Etta's ex-husband and our mother." Everyone gasps around us, Lani walks to Etta holding her tight.

Everyone knows our story, it's never been a secret. I watch as everyone slowly connects the dots as to what is happening and what this means.

Shaylin looks to everyone on the bus and tears out of it in a full-blown sprint with Raven right on her ass. Everyone else follows suit leaving Etta and I alone together.

I take her hand and we follow after them confused as to what they are doing. Shaylin walks straight up to the front door, kicks it in and runs straight in with the girls right on her ass.

Etta is pale, I have not seen her like this since we were kids when she was told she had to marry Michael. We walk inside the house and I hold onto her tighter wanting her to know that I'm there for her.

The sight before me will be forever ingrained in the back of my eyelids. My mother is on her knees in front of Michael. He pushes her off, stuffing himself back in his pants when everyone busts inside of the house. His eyes settle on Etta, his face showing his shock that she is standing in front of him after all these years.

Then his face morphs into his true self- pure and vile evil. He is depravity and it's written all over his face, the one I have seen many times before he turns to take it out on someone.

Shaylin steps in front of Etta blocking his gaze from her. "Get them!" she yells and everyone charges at once except me, Etta, Adeline, and Bell who wraps their arms around Etta comforting her as we watch the scene unfold.

Shaylin punches him square in the face. His face flies back from the hit and River goes straight for my mother dragging her by her hair. Shaylin grips him by the back of his head, slamming his face into the coffee table hard. River is ripping handfuls of hair out of my mother's head as she's screaming, crying, and begging for her to let her go.

I don't have any regrets, they treated us like slaves. They are nothing to me. I used to feel sorry for her, but now? I feel absolute hate at the way she has treated us.

We assumed she was a victim of her circumstance; we even gave her a get out of jail free card. We left her, let her live all of those years ago. I even felt sorry for her. No, she is just as fucked up as the rest of them. I want her to pay for the way she has treated Etta and my brothers.

Michael screams loudly and I jump from the sound. He pushes Shaylin off of him and she smacks into the ground on her backside. She recovers quickly, standing.

He looks at Etta, his face so angry it takes my breath away. Etta doesn't even flinch giving him back the same glare he is giving her.

She is back.

"I am coming back for you, Jezebel. Watch your back," he threatens her right in front of all of us. Michael turns and sprints toward the back of the house and we hear a door opening and closing, assuming he ran outside. He has been here in town all of this time and we didn't even know it.

Our mother crawls on her hands and knees toward the direction that he went. "Don't leave me, baby!" she screams for him, like he's going to come back for her.

Amelia walks over to us. "I think it's time we call the guys."

The prospect runs inside the house and he doesn't come in with Michael, they didn't even come inside as everything went down. Useless.

I take out my phone and move away from Etta so she doesn't hear my conversation, all ignoring the crying of our egg donor on the floor rolling around. I call Konrad first, I give him a basic run down of what happened. I can hear the bike start as he hangs up.

Then I call Tristan. "Hi baby, are you okay?" he asks.

I close my eyes at the sound of his voice and the feelings he brings out of me. "Shit has been really bad tonight, Tristan. We decided to egg some cult member's houses and a couple came out of one of the houses. It was my mom and Michael, Etta's ex-husband," I explain to him as fast as I can because I want to get back to Etta.

I am still in shock that this happened.

Years ago, Vinny, Trey, and Lani came and got us; I was sixteen and Etta was eighteen. We let our mother go because our dad was horrible, he was horrible to everyone. We thought she would be spending the rest of her life alone.

I always had this weird feeling when Michael and our mom were around each other. They would give each other secret looks; once my dad caught her and she was punished severely.

Why did she push Etta into marrying Michael so much? She forced her by her hair literally to the altar and I couldn't do anything about it.

I hear their bikes before I see them and I feel a rush of relief knowing that the guys will be here.

Konrad is the first in the door, he stops in his tracks when he sees Etta staring at the ground.

I bite my lip holding back my tears, I wish that this didn't happen to her. She is so strong and it's hard to see her so hurt and down; she takes care of everyone, tries to protect everyone.

Vinny steps in front of Konrad in shock at the sight of our mother lying there, crying for Michael. "Mom?" he says in disbelief.

Trey hisses with anger. I can see him shaking from across the room where I am standing next to Etta.

Etta gathers herself and I squeeze her hand letting her know I am here for her. "We were trashing this house when they walked outside; my mother and Michael, together. The girls ran in here and beat them up," she explains with a void of emotion in her voice.

I swallow hard, fighting back the tears. "He said that he is coming back for me, he threatened me." Her voice cracks at the last part.

Konrad looks like he's going to murder everyone but at the same time, his face is showing his softness for my sister. "Angel." He slowly walks to her pulling her to his chest, I can see her whole body sinking into him.

I let go of her hand knowing that I am not needed anymore, she's in good hands. I smile at Konrad, patting his shoulder so thankful the way he is with my sister.

He pulls back, so she's looking up at him. "I love you, baby. You are safe with me, always." He kisses her forehead and she closes her eyes.

The tears break loose watching them together. Our mom on the floor is practically screaming at this point wanting Michael to come back to her, to save her.

Tristan runs through the door. "Who has Michaela?" I ask him.

He pulls me into him, holding me tight. Like he needed to hold me. "My dad and Summer are with her. I came to get you."

Trey scowls at me and Etta with our guys, I cover my smile. Trey is our brother-in-law technically but he has taken his role as our protector seriously.

I hear a sharp scream and look down to see Shaylin lifting our mother to her knees so she is facing everyone. She looks at me and Etta, her eyes red from crying and she looks absolutely awful like she's on drugs or she's starving herself. She moves forward on her knees toward Etta. Tristan tightens his grip on me like he's ready to wrench me out of the way.

She lifts her hands like she is begging. "Etta, don't let them kill me," she pleads.

Etta steps away from Konrad, going to her and she grips her face hard, her fingers digging into her face. "You do not speak to me. I could kill you myself, but I won't. That's going to be left up to someone else. You are nothing, you are a piece of shit who only cared about herself."

I am so proud of Etta right now for standing up to her, she needed to do this, she needed to take a piece back of what they had taken from her.

She pulls herself from Etta's grip, glaring at her. "How dare you speak to me this way! I am your mother and you will help me!" she screeches before she turns her eyes to me.

It sickens me that I have the same eyes as her. "My sweet daughter, come help me please. I was good to you," she pleads to me, fake tears in her eyes.

What I feel is nothing, I shake my head no to her. "You forced marriage upon me when I was thirteen years old to a man that was over twice my age. You are not my mother. You let others hurt me, you didn't protect me. You gave birth to me and

143

that's it." She is shocked that I said anything back to her, I'm not the same little girl I was back then.

She turns back to Etta to plead with her once more but Konrad steps in front of her, gripping Etta by her hair. "You will not look at her again or I will rip your eyes out from their sockets and make you eat them, bitch. Do you understand me?" he growls at her.

Tristan steps in front of me. "Konrad is a better man than me, I won't share what the fuck I will do to you if you dare to look at my woman again." He is vibrating with anger.

She looks crestfallen knowing that we are not going to help her so she goes to her last resort, Vinny. "Please, Vinny, help your momma. I beg you, son." Vinny just looks sick to his stomach.

Lani takes over. "You do not speak to him. You think I don't know what you have done, bitch? Do you all know this woman loved it when her kids were being hurt so she could watch it happen?" Lani admits to everyone in the room.

I close my eyes and look at the ground as old memories come back to me, some that I want to forget more than anything. I wish the abuse started when I was married but no, it started a long time before that and it happened with all of my siblings.

Tristan steps in front of me, hiding me from my mother. "Baby, don't hide your eyes from me," he begs me, rubbing my cheekbones to get my attention.

I smile at him but it's hard to not feel the same no matter how much you tell yourself it's not your fault. It's just there and it never goes away.

"Shaylin, can you handle this?" Konrad asks.

Just as we are getting ready to leave, we hear a sharp cry from the back of the house and I look at everyone in shock because it sounds like a small baby. Etta takes off running and we all follow her to where the cry came from. She pushes open a bedroom door, inside a crib is a newborn baby. Oh my God.

Tristan curses under his breath, my motherly instincts kick in and I reach inside of the crib to pick him up tucking him to my chest. I look at Tristan my heart shattering at the sight of him; he does not look good at all. His diaper is so huge, it's hanging to his feet. The baby looks as though he has not been bathed in quite a long time. Worse yet, he looks to be a preemie or a very malnourished baby.

Tristan looks just as heartbroken as I do. He starts digging inside of the drawers looking for a diaper. He finds one and I set him down onto the changing table getting him cleaned up as best as I can.

I use a clean baby wipe and clean his face, under his neck as best as I can until he can get a bath. Tristan hands me a new onesie and I hurry putting it on him since it's really cold in here.

I lift him, snuggling him to my chest. Tristan puts his hand on the back of his head, staring down at him. He is an absolutely beautiful baby. I smile putting my hand on Tristan's.

We walk into the living room and our mother glares at us. "Well, I guess you found him," she deadpans like it's no big deal.

I am pissed off, more than I have ever been in my life. "He's in horrible shape, he hasn't been bathed and he hasn't been properly fed. How could you do this?" My voice cracks at the end showing how affected I am by this.

My mother just shrugs her shoulders. "I didn't want him but I wasn't going to let him starve. I raised you guys. I didn't have help. That's why I was here trying to get Michael to help me raise him."

My mind is boggled, how someone could be this evil I truly don't understand. She looks at me and Etta like it's all our fault, like we are the cause of all of her problems.

I look down at his beautiful sweet face and I make a rash decision but I know it's one that I will never regret as soon as the words leave my mouth. "I will raise him as my own. He's my brother," I announce to everyone in the room.

Tristan's arm tightens around my back. I peek up at him and he is nodding to me letting me know that he is in the same boat as me, that I have his support.

Etta walks to me. "I will help you, anytime," Vinny joins. "I guess we have a baby brother. We will do it together." He shows his support.

The moment is interrupted by our egg donor screeching, "Well, isn't this beautiful! You're taking my son from me!" She tries to get up like she's going to take him from us.

Shaylin comes up from behind her and punches her in the mouth. "Why don't you shut the fuck up? You're ruining the moment, bitch."

"Shaylin, you still good handling this?" Konrad confirms. Shaylin agrees with the help of the other ladies.

Tristan leads me out of the house as the sounds of our mother screaming at the top of her lungs demanding for us to come back, that we can't do this to her.

I don't look back because I feel absolutely nothing.

13

LYNN

I AM SITTING in the warm truck with the baby, while Tristan is inside the store getting some emergency supplies until I can go shopping.

One of the guys lent us their infant car seat until we can get our own which I am thankful for.

On our way to the store, it dawned on us that my mom made no mention of the baby's name.

"Zane, you look like a Zane," I tell him, snuggling him. He's fussy, I know he must be hungry. She didn't even have any formula in the house.

I lift him, pressing him against my chest. I love him, the second I saw him in the crib I knew that he was mine. And I have no doubt that Michaela is going to be over the moon about him.

The back door opens and Tristan sets bags on top of bags in the back seat. "I got a bassinet too. The worker is loading it in the back for us," Tristan tells me and I am relieved.

I hand him the baby and he puts him back in his car seat gently, staring into his little face.

I love him, I love the way he just accepted that we were going to take in my baby brother as ours. But I need to ask him, I need to make sure that he is on board with everything and that he wants to do this.

Once everything is loaded in the truck, he gets up front and starts on the drive home. "Tristan, you know that I am giving you a get out of a jail free card. You don't have to do this."

His face shows his shock at my words. "What? Fuck no, baby. I'm with you one hundred percent. He is ours, just like Michaela is mine."

Fuck. The tears can't be stopped, I feel relief that I never knew that I needed. I needed to hear those words.

I lean over and rest my forehead on his shoulder overwhelmed by everything. "God, I love you so much," I admit to him, I press my hand on his thigh overwhelmed by how much I feel for him.

He kisses the top of my head. "I love you too, so much. I'm with you one hundred percent, no matter what."

"Zane. How do you feel about calling him Zane?" I ask.

Tristan smiles reaching over and squeezing my thigh. "I like that."

We arrive back home and I see Walker and Michaela both standing at the front door looking out.

"Does Michaela know?" I ask Tristan. She is currently jumping up and down like it's Christmas morning.

He nods. "Yeah, I asked dad to give her a rundown so it's not a total shock."

I giggle at her antics as Walker picks her up so she can see better and walks out onto the porch. "Mommy, do I have a baby brother?" she yells.

Tristan's on cloud nine. He reaches into the back seat and takes out Zane in his car seat.

"Oh yea, before I forget, Myra is coming over to check him

out," I tell Tristan. I need to get him looked over as soon as possible, we can see that she hasn't really taken care of him. I know it's late but I need to know or I won't sleep at all.

"Good idea," Tristan agrees.

Walker walks in the house with Michaela and sets her down on the ground. Tristan sets the car seat down in front of her so she can look at him.

She puts her little hand to her mouth, gasping. "Oh my God, he is so precious!" she says dramatically while rubbing his little cheek.

I smile at her, happy that she is so happy with it, not that I had any doubt.

"Sweetheart," I get her attention, "he is actually my little brother but I am going to be taking care of him like I do you. Are you okay with that?" I ask her, wanting to make sure.

Her wide eyes go from me to Zane. "I mean he will be my baby brother anyway, Mommy."

That lets me know that she is definitely fine with it.

"I am going to bring everything in," Tristan tells me, Walker gets up to help him.

"Mommy, why is his hair dirty?" she wonders.

My heart breaks that she even noticed that. Taking her hand, I tell her, "Baby, he was not in a good home before we got him tonight. We need to take extra good care of him so he gets better."

She gives me the saddest, heartbreaking look I have ever seen. "Mommy, why would anyone not be nice to him?"

I pull her into my lap. "I am not sure sweetheart, but he's with us now and that is what matters." I kiss her temple and unbuckle him from his seat. "We need to give him a bath and get him fed, want to help me?" I ask her.

The sadness is gone in her eyes. "Yes! I want that!" She jumps up and claps her hands together.

Tristan returns from outside and sets a pile of bags down onto the floor and Michaela digs in them getting out the supplies. She finds a cute little pajama onesie. "Wow, I think he needs to wear this tonight." Then she pulls out the bottles, water, and formula for him setting them on the table.

"Mommy, should we go wash these bottles? It says here we should." She points to the writing on the back. She's so smart.

"We will, sweetheart."

I reach inside and take out his bath stuff and a new diaper. We don't have a bathtub. "We will bathe him in the sink tonight."

Walker puts the bassinet box on the floor. "I will put this together as you guys get the little man sorted."

"Thank you so much, Walker."

He gives me that smile that reminds me so much of Tristan. "Ready?" Tristan asks and takes him from me. I stand up and Michaela runs into the kitchen with an armload of stuff.

"She is taking this really well," he tells me as we walk together to the kitchen.

"She is, that makes me happy."

I turn on the water letting it warm up before I stuff a few towels in the bottom of the sink and grab another towel to put under his head and arms to hold him out of the water.

I help Tristan take him out of his clothes and I just throw them straight in the trash.

"Look at his little hands!" Michaela takes his little fingers wiggling them. She's sitting on the counter next to the sink.

Tristan sets him gently in the water, he kicks his little legs making a little splash. "Aww," I sigh.

I start on his hair as Tristan keeps a tight grip on him so he doesn't fall in the water. I scrub him head to toe making sure he's squeaky clean.

Michaela holds up a towel for him. Tristan lifts him out of

the water and hands him to her. I, of course, secretly help her as she holds him.

Tristan and I share a secret smile as she coos at him and rocks him. I hear the front door open and we look over to see to Myra there with Mia and Ryan.

"Hi guys, thank you for coming," I tell them. Michaela gets excited to see Mia who is a little older than her.

"Of course, let me see the little fellow." Myra smiles and takes him from Michaela, laying him on the counter so she can check him over.

"He is definitely underweight, but otherwise he seems healthy. The real test is going to be labs and I assume that he hasn't had any of his shots but for right now I am going to draw some blood." I cringe at the sight of the needle when she brings it out.

Michaela takes a tight hold of his hand, holding it close to her. "It will be over in just a second," she promises.

"The bassinet is done. Where do you want me to put it?" Walker asks.

"Our room, Dad. Thank you," Tristan answers for me.

"Mia, you're growing up on us!" I lean over and hug her, she's a spitting image of her mother.

She smiles and takes Ryan's hand, she's a daddy's girl that's for sure. Tristan takes my hand as Zane starts to cry from the needle.

"How old do you think he is?" I ask her.

She studies him for a moment. "Honestly I think he is a little less than a month old."

"Alright I am done here. I will send this off and in the morning, I will have the results if you guys will come into my office?" she asks.

"We will be there, just text us the time. Thank you so much for coming." I take her spot and put on his diaper, diaper cream for the horrible rash from being left in his diaper way too long, and his new pajamas. "Well, isn't he so cute." I admire him smoothing his little bit of hair over to the side.

"He is so cute," Michaela agrees.

He starts to cry and loudly. "I think it's time we feed him," Tristan tells us and takes the bottles to the sink to clean them.

"I'll be in the living room," I tell him and Michaela follows close to me. I sit down and grab the container of formula looking at how much to feed him. Michaela was breastfed, I never had to deal with formula so it's new territory for me.

"Mommy, can I hold him?"

She sits back and I grab a Boppy Pillow that Tristan bought, wrapping it around her so she can hold him easier. I gently set him in her arms and she glows.

She puts her finger in his hand and he wraps his tiny fingers around her one. "Mommy, he's holding my finger," she squeals.

I kiss her cheek. "He loves you, sweet girl."

She looks like I just gave her the world. Tristan walks into the living room and he takes in the scene, his face so serene as he takes the both of them in.

I take the bottle from him and fill it with water adding the formula. "Alright, honey. I am going to feed him and then you can have him back after you get ready for bed," I tell Michaela and as soon as I have him in my arms, she takes off like a light upstairs so she can hurry back.

Tristan settles in next to me as I press the bottle to his lips and he latches on, drinking as fast as he can.

"Who would have thought today would have turned out like this?" I joke and he laughs. "But I am happy with the way it turned out, even if I am so fucking angry with the way he has been mistreated."

My heart breaks once again as I think about it. I lean over and rest my head on his shoulder as he drinks. "I think we need to wake him up every few hours even if he sleeps because he needs to eat as much as possible."

"That is a good idea."

"Do you want to feed him while I go check on her?" I ask.

He lifts his hands and I hand him over; he looks so tiny in Tristan's arms. He looks so completely natural holding him.

I hand over a blanket covering up Zane so he is warm. "I'll be upstairs if you want to come on up once he's finished."

I grab the bottles that Tristan has cleaned, the water, and formula so we won't have to run up and down the stairs. Walker comes out of the bathroom just as I pass scaring the shit out of me. "Oh my God, I forgot you were here," I tell him, holding my heart.

He laughs and gives me a hug. "I'm leaving now though, I need to get back to my girl." I love the way happy looks on him.

"I am sure Darren is taking good care of her." His smile grows even wider at that. "We will have to babysit Michaela and that little one sometime. You know Summer will be chomping at the bit."

He gives me a fatherly kiss on the top of my head before he walks to Tristan telling him goodbye.

Michaela is brushing her teeth when I find her. "Tristan will be in soon to read you a goodnight story."

"Oh I better find which one I want to read tonight." She runs to her bookshelf and sits down on the floor to find the perfect one.

A few minutes later Tristan walks in holding Zane. He gently hands him to Michaela so she can hold him as we read the story to her. I have never felt contentment like this in my life until this very moment, watching all of them together.

"Goodnight, sweet girl." I take the baby from her and Tristan tucks her in. "Sleep good, angel."

She closes her eyes and rolls over with a smile on her face.

We pull her door shut and walk into our bedroom, exhaustion hits me the second I see the bed. "I'm so tired, today has been such a long day."

"Go get in the shower sweetheart, I will join you in a few minutes." No matter how tired I am I can't pass that up.

I strip out of my clothes, groaning at the feel of the warm water beating on my back. I rest my forehead against the tile basking in the few minutes I have alone to gather my thoughts on what has gone down today.

Arms wrap around me from behind and I lean my head back against his warm chest. He doesn't speak, he just holds me and lets me have this moment.

I turn around and wrap my arm around him wanting to be closer. "We can do this."

I nod against his chest. "I will take care of all of you always." He lifts my head so he can kiss me. I can never doubt the way he loves me from the way his lips move against mine. His lips slowly stroke mine, lovingly, I can feel it down to my toes. His hands go to my ass lifting me off the floor, my legs curl around him. I'm aching for him.

"I want you."

He presses his forehead against mine, holding my face gently. "You have me, always."

He shifts my body and I close my eyes as he slowly slides inside of me, there's nothing like the feeling of being filled by him. I throw my head back, bumping it against the tile as he works me up and down on him. The only sounds in the shower are the sounds of our slapping skin, the water, and our moans.

"God," I moan, clenching down on him. His hands tighten on my hips, pulling me down harder and deeper. My hands slap the shower wall trying to grip onto something.

All of a sudden, he stops moving and he pulls me off him, turns me around and bends over in the shower. I turn around to look at him just as he slams back inside of me.

"FUCK." I bite my lip trying not to wake everyone up in the house.

His hand fists my wet hair, pulling me back with his thrusts. My legs are shaking, I'm burning.

I face plant into the shower walls, the sensations becoming too overwhelming. He reaches under me rubbing my clit with his thrusts.

I bang my fist into the wall, the rising inferno, I'm so close but it feels so far away.

Smack! His hand lands on my ass cheek and I jolt, clenching down onto him hard. My legs give out and I fall to the shower floor, as I fall apart, shaking and convulsing.

He keeps on moving, holding my legs open as he continues to pound into me harder and harder. My body is not my own right now, it belongs to him to do as he pleases.

His hand slams down onto the shower floor as he comes inside of me and I follow him again over the edge.

He slides out of me and falls to the bottom of the shower next to me as the warm water rains down next to us. I look at him, his eyes are closed and he is trying to control his breathing. I don't have any control of my body anymore.

"We are lying on the shower floor," I point out and he busts out laughing and I join in.

He pushes himself up off the floor, helping me up with him. I lean against the wall, my legs are still like Jello-O.

He washes me gently, taking extra care of my breasts. I smack his hand away and he grins to himself looking proud.

"Your cut came in."

My heart does that little dance. "You ordered one for me? Oh wow!" In the biker world this is a huge deal.

He turns off the water wrapping me in a towel, he walks out of the room into our bedroom and comes back with a box.

"Tristan," I say softly, feeling emotional.

He kisses the side of my head and I open the box, touching the patch that says "Property of Tristan."

"I love you." I kiss his chest and wrap my arms around him, his hands rub down my back. "I love you angel, one day soon I'm going to put that ring on your finger and I am going to put my babies in your stomach."

I lean back at that, shocked that he said that. "You want more babies?" I ask, trying not to get excited.

He shows me those beautiful dimples. "Fuck yeah. I want to see you barefoot and pregnant in my kitchen, woman." He smacks my bare ass and I push him away laughing.

"Well, I guess I will just throw out my birth control," I joke, putting some face lotion on and finish getting ready for bed.

He is staring at me in the mirror. "Fuck, I did that yesterday," he tells me seriously.

I look at him in shock. "Wait, is that why I couldn't find it earlier?" I ask.

He nods looking way too proud of himself. "You're crazy."

He laughs, shrugging his shoulder like that doesn't bother him at all. "Well, I am crazy about you, darlin." He rubs my bare cheek and I shake my head at his craziness.

I can say over and over how crazy he is but in the end, I love every single second of it.

I pick up the shirt he brought into the bathroom for me slipping it over my head and slipping on a pair of underwear.

"Okay," I agree.

He turns me around, lifting me up on the counter so I'm tall enough to be face to face with him. "You don't know how happy you just made me; I want a house full of little angels."

I drop my head to his chest, snuggling into him. "I want a little Tristan who is just like his daddy." I feel his smile where his lips are at the top of my head. He sets me on the floor and I yawn, tired.

"I'm beat, we probably need to go to sleep before the little one wakes up." I walk out of the bathroom and I peek into his bassinet where Zane is sleeping peacefully. I rub his little cheek, my heart warm.

"I promise to give you a good life sweetheart, to take care of you and most of all, I will love you," I promise to him.

I know my mother is dead and I don't have one ounce of guilt about that, she was a horrible person. It's one thing to live through how horribly she was treated when I was younger, but I am older now. I am a mother and the way she has treated Zane will give me nightmares.

I slide into bed and Tristan turns on the fan we use for noise. "Goodnight, baby," he whispers, kissing my cheek.

"Goodnight, love you," I mumble, snuggling deeper into him.

A SHARP CRY brings me out of my dream and I sit up gasping holding my chest as the alarm goes off at the same time.

Tristan lifts Zane out of the bassinet that is next to him. "Shh, it's okay," Tristan whispers to him, holding the back of his head rocking him slightly.

I reach over onto the nightstand and make him a bottle, turning off the alarm and resetting it.

I hand the bottle to Tristan, he turns him into the crook of his arm and presses the bottle in his mouth. "There, that's better." He rubs the top of his little head.

My poor heart, I'm not sure if I can take it. I lean back against the pillow watching him feed Zane. Just when you think you can't love someone else more than you already do, you see another side of them and fall even deeper.

I gather Zane's diapers, wipes, and more butt cream; I want to change him as often as possible to keep his butt dry and get rid of that diaper rash.

I miss Michaela being this little, she was the cuddliest baby.

At nighttime after my husband was done with me and went to his bedroom, I would roll over and hold her hand all night long.

To think that I was thirteen years old when I was married and that is around Tiffany's age. It doesn't hit you how young you were until you see someone the same age you were when you got married.

That life was so horrible, I am so thankful that Michaela wasn't raised in that life. I am so blessed that I get this happily ever after.

Tristan burps him. "He was hungry." He wipes his little mouth with a burp cloth and he hands him off to me to change his diaper.

"Now that's better," I tell him after I change his diaper and put his pacifier in his mouth, his eyes are already closed. "Do you want to put him in?" I whisper.

He lifts him and sets him gently into the bassinet and I fall back into bed closing my eyes. I almost died when I had Michaela. I was so young it was not healthy. I was in labor for such a long time. They didn't believe in c-sections in the cult, so I struggled to deliver her.

If you are on your period in the cult, they would lock you inside your bedroom because we weren't to be seen that way; we were failing as women because that means we were without child.

A woman's life duties were to have babies and raise them. If you couldn't produce babies, then that means your life was hell.

That's why Etta's life was a living hell; she was never able to conceive a child. "What has you thinking so hard?" Tristan asks in the darkness of the room.

I turn over and rest my head on his shoulder. "I'm just thinking of the life we used to live in the cult. Seeing Zane brought back some old memories."

He hugs me to him. "I'm sorry, I wish that you never had to experience any of that."

"I'm so glad that Michaela never has to experience any of that," I tell him, my heart hurting just from the thoughts of it.

"I hired someone to track down Lee," he tells me in the darkness of the room.

"You did?" I ask.

I can feel my skin crawling at even just his name.

"Yeah, it's time to end him once and for all."

God, I sure hope so.

1 4

LYNN

ONE MONTH LATER

"Tristan, he just smiled at me!" Michaela yells from the living room, we're in the kitchen making dinner before we head to her volleyball game.

We both smile at each other. I was seriously afraid that she was going to be jealous of him, but she falls more in love with him every single day.

Plus, I don't think she has time to get jealous considering the fact everyone dotes on her especially Walker; she is papa's girl as she says. I love that for her, she spends at least one night a week with them.

Zane is an absolute chunk now; he's thriving and I am so pleased with that. "What time is her game again?" Tristan asks, holding his cell phone.

"Seven." I put some carrots on Michaela's plate.

"Dad is coming and he is wanting to know if he can keep both of the kids tonight." Tristan wiggles his eyebrows.

I laugh. "Yea, that's fine."

Tristan walks to me, putting his hand on my ass. "Good. It's time to make us a baby."

He's still, with all of his effort, trying to get me knocked up.

160

"Mommy, how do you make a baby?" Michaela asks out of nowhere.

I panic and drop the pan on Tristan's hand on the counter. He yells and sticks his hand under the water to stop the burning. Sweat pools at the back of my neck, Tristan looks like he is going to pass out. "Well, sweetheart. When a man loves a woman..."

Her eyes widen and then she screams at the top of her lungs holding her stomach, "Mom a boy at school said he loved me at recess, I'm pregnant. I just know it." She falls to the floor sobbing dramatically.

Tristan is looking like he is going to pass out. "What the fu... Who is that guy's parent!" Tristan corrects himself, picking her up off of the floor. She falls to his shoulder crying.

"Sweetheart, you are not pregnant. Remember how I said it's when a MAN and WOMAN love each other, not a little boy and a little girl?" I try to come up with a solution.

She lifts her head sniffing, wiping under her eyes. "Are you sure?" she asks me.

Tristan looks like he's going to murder everyone in sight, I'm going to have a heart attack because I wasn't prepared for this yet. No parent wants their kid to ask them such things.

"I am positive," I reassure her.

She wipes her hand over the back of her forehead. "Phew goodness, I was scared for a second. I love Zane but a girl needs her sleep," she says in a way that is too old for her age.

Tristan sets her down laughing. "You are my baby girl, no babies for you until you're sixty."

"Oh stop it, Daddy." She giggles and runs off.

Fuck.

Tristan leans against the counter, now I think he is the one that is having a heart attack.

"Did she just?" he asks.

I nod, pressing my hands to my mouth not wanting her to hear me because now I want to cry.

He presses his hand to his heart. "Fuck, baby." He smiles, this is the happiest I have ever seen him. He loves her so much. I just know that he will never forget this moment ever in his life.

He may not have helped create her, but she is his in every other way. He gets her up in the morning, takes her to school as I stay home with Zane. Practically coaches her volleyball team since the second she said she wanted to play.

He is amazing.

"She loves you."

His eyes look misty and he looks down at the floor. "Fuck, she's in my heart in a way that I didn't think was possible. I love all of you. You guys are all of me."

I kiss him softly, my tears mingling with the kiss. I literally cry at the drop of a hat these days. He kisses me gently once more and we gather our food bringing it to the dining room table.

I check on Zane in his little bouncer in the living room to make sure he's good. "Come on sweet boy, time for your dinner." I pick him up out of the bouncer.

"I will make the bottle." Michaela is a pro at this point, she always wants to feed him.

Tristan rubs the top of Zane's head and Michaela sets the bottle down onto the table in front of me and sits down digging into the chicken.

"Papa bear wants you to stay all night with him tonight," I tell her.

She smacks her hands together. "Ohh I can't wait, Darren promised I could dress him up next time I came to stay."

Tristan chuckles and hands me a bite of chicken before taking a bite of his own. "I think your papa bear and Darren have made you a spoiled rotten little girl." She gives me a sheepish look.

I can't say anything about it because I have her spoiled too and don't get me started on Tristan. Their little date day has become a monthly thing where he takes her out.

"Are they coming to my game?" she asks.

"They are and you will go home with them from there if you want."

She nods enthusiastically. "I would love that, Summer is my friend." My heart warms at that. Summer was just her therapist for a while, strictly professional, but now they are so close.

"I'm so ready to kick some booty tonight." Michaela slams her hand down onto the table gently before making a tiny fist waving it in the air.

Tristan covers his mouth so she doesn't see his smile. "Wow, I bet they will be terrified tonight, they may quit before the game even starts."

She nods her head in agreement. "That would be a perk, poor things." She sighs dramatically like she feels sorry for them.

She is so cute.

THE GAME IS PACKED when we leave the locker rooms to join the crowd. We stand at the entrance to the court to see if we see Walker, Darren, and Summer.

Tristan is holding baby Zane to his chest in a little carrier which is absolutely adorable. The carrier is so little and Tristan is so huge. He has one hand at the bottom of Zane's bottom and the diaper bag in the other. I tried to help him but he wouldn't let me.

I see someone waving. "There they are!" I tell Tristan and we make our way over to them.

Tristan puts his hand on the small of my back, while holding the diaper bag, leading me through the throes of many parents.

"Finally." I sigh as soon as my butt touches the seats. "Ohh can I hold him?" Summer asks, peeking over Tristan's shoulder to see inside of the carrier.

"Sure can." I take him out and wrap him in a blanket since it's drafty in here with the door opening and closing as people move in and out.

She takes him, snuggling him to her chest. I turn my head away when I see the look Walker and Darren give her.

"Which one of those is the dad of the little boy who told Michaela he loved her?" Tristan mumbles under his breath, eyeing every one of them to see if they show any sign of them being that dad.

I pat his leg at his ridiculousness. "What did I hear about someone telling Michaela they loved her?" Darren asks and Tristan turns around gladly to explain the situation, both of them getting fired up about it.

"Well, we need to find that fucking dad so we can set him straight," Darren growls.

I shake my head not even looking at them because they are ridiculous. But I can't help but find it hilarious that they are so caught up in it.

The locker doors open and I start clapping when I see Michaela walking out of the door stretching her arms back and forth.

"Look at that baby," Walker says and I hear the sound of his camera going off.

"Woohoo! Go Michaela," a young voice says and I watch in sync as Tristan, Darren, and Walker eye him then to the dad next to him.

Well, this is no good.

Michaela looks at him and turns away, her face red from the attention. "I do not love you Ronald, you almost got me pregnant!" she yells to him in the crowd and turns away dismissing him.

Well, if I think I could die on the spot, it would be in this very moment. Tristan is hiding his face in disbelief and all I can do is stare into the same spot praying no one else heard that.

"Tristan, how will I recover from this?" I groan, rubbing my eyes before I bust out laughing at what she said, my poor heart won't make it until she is a teenager.

Tristan joins in laughing with me. I look at the little boy down below us and he is pouting, my guess is she broke his little heart.

Yeah, I am not ready for this life, I don't think Tristan can make it through her dating.

"What the fuck did she just say?" Walker says and we burst out laughing again.

HER GAME WAS OVER QUICK, Michaela is really talented at soft-ball and volleyball. She has been practicing so much and it's paying off.

"You did so good, my girl!" I hug her when she runs up to us holding her bag. She grins and shakes me side to side, hugging me excitedly.

Tristan lifts her off the ground squeezing her. "I'm so proud of you." He kisses her cheek. "Thank you." She pats his cheeks.

He sets her down and takes her hand not letting her go far. "You ready to come to our house?" Walker tugs on her hair getting her attention.

She claps her hands together. "I am so excited, can we watch *Halloween Town?*"

Darren rubs the top of her head. "We can do whatever you want, sweetheart." Summer is just watching them both, swooning over them both as am I. It's an amazing sight to see such scary looking men be so taken by Michaela.

I reach over and take Zane from Summer wanting to get my

snuggles in before they take him away.

"I will miss you, baby boy." I breathe in his sweet baby scent before handing him back off to Tristan to say goodbye then I pull Michaela wanting to love on her. "I love you, baby; have fun and I will see you tomorrow." I squeeze her tight before handing her off to Tristan so he can say goodbye.

"Oh yeah Lynn, the client who called me about you has sent her folder to me. It's on my desk if you want to stop by and get it?" she asks me. We sometimes work together on cases and this one requested me specially for what I specialize in.

"That's a good idea, I can look it over on the way home." I take the key that Summer hands out to me.

"Be good for your papa bear," I tell Michaela and she's not fazed as she takes his hand. "We are going to have the most fun." She tugs on his arm wanting to get out of here.

"Bye, guys!" I call to them as they walk through the doors, hurting a little not wanting them to go, Zane hasn't left very often and it's hard for him to do so.

"Let's go home and make some babies now," Tristan whispers in my ear.

I giggle and pull back, my face red from him saying this in front of a bunch of people.

I almost forget to stop at Summer's office on the way back home. Tristan is in a hurry to put a baby in me.

"I will be right back." I walk to the front door and let myself inside turning on the light.

I always hate going to new places in the dark, ghosts terrify me. I spot the folder on top of the desk exactly where she told me.

I open the folder to take a peek and I almost drop it when I see the face of the person looking back at me.

My mother's picture, who's dead.

"Well, it took long enough to get you alone." I turn around and come to face to face with Lee.

15

LYNN

I TAKE a step back until my back hits the desk. I try not to panic as I look into the face of the man who has caused hell in mine and my daughter's life.

"What are you doing here?" I ask him, playing it off like it's no big deal.

He grins. "You know exactly why I'm here. I am here to get my fiancée and you are going to bring her to me. You are a hard woman to get alone. I created this fake ruse then I waited for you to show up. Smart, huh?"

My stomach burns with the anger I am feeling, how dare he do this? She is a baby.

"She is not your fiancée, you sick fuck. She is a baby!" I tell him with such ferocity only a mother can muster, I'm sickened by his presence. I want to shake him, kill him, just about anything to work out this aggression he causes by being alive.

He tuts at me, waggling his finger leaning against the wall. "She is mine, God has spoken to me about it. She's young, but she will be of age in a few years. But we are not here to discuss this. I'm here to take my fiancée home and I found you a new proper husband so we can fix these..." He looks me up and down with disgust. "These obedience issues of yours."

My brain is going a hundred miles an hour, trying to wrap my head around the fact that he is standing here in front of me and the bullshit he is spewing.

I try to think of a plan to get Tristan's attention. I have had nightmares over this, seeing him again.

"Lee, do you not understand how insane this is? What you are suggesting? She is an eight-year-old little girl. This is not rational," I try to explain to him, hoping he gets the insanity of this.

He shakes his head side to side like a child throwing a tantrum and he throws his fists up to his face like he is fighting himself. He throws his arm out pointing at me. "You are the one who is fighting God, you are the one who is not rational," he screams and I mean loudly.

I think he's losing his mind. His hands go back to his face smacking himself before he stops, his hands falling beside him. He looks over to a set of doors that leads deeper into the office. I follow his gaze and see an old man dressed in all white.

"This is my father. He has decided that he must take on the mission of reverting you back to God's will. He's here to take you home and I get my Michaela," Lee says in a soft, blissful voice as he looks at his father like the world sets on him.

His father looks at me, his eyes moving from my toes all the way up to the top of my head. "She will definitely do; I see the devil in her but it can all be worked out. Do not worry, son." He pats him on the shoulder in a comforting manner.

I want to throw up, I just want to run out of here and leave. Both of them are staring at me like I'm the last meal on earth.

"We can see where Michaela gets her good looks from. We hope that the devil is not in her." He sighs like this is a hardship on him.

"The only people that have the devil in them are the both of you, you are both sick in the head. She is eight years old. How can you even fathom the things you are saying?"

Lee's father turns to me in disgust. "She is worse off than I thought, we must save her immediately before it bleeds to Michaela." He ignores me, talking to Lee.

Lee nods his head in agreement. "We must save her, she's too important to allow this low born Satanist to destroy her life."

What the fuck are they even saying? They aren't making any sense. Do they think of themselves as royalty?

Lee's father walks to me, stopping a few feet away. I step back until the back of my legs are touching the desk. "Where is she? You must tell us where Michaela is this instant," he demands of me.

He reaches forward before I can move, gripping my arms hard and shaking me. "Tell us now!" he screams in my face, losing all his fake composure.

I shake my head no, staring him dead in the eye; I am not afraid to look at the devil in the flesh. I am not thirteen years old anymore. I smile. I would rather die than tell them where she is. "I will never tell you."

He glares at me, looking back at Lee. "Well, I guess that means we have to make her."

Lee grins at me. "I would love to have first taste." Then he charges me.

Tristan

I LOOK at the doors to Summer's office wondering where Lynn is, it shouldn't be taking this long for her to get a folder. Worried, I get out of the truck and walk to the front door. Standing outside of it I can hear loud voices from the inside.

What the fuck?

I push open the door just as Lynn screams my name.

I follow the direction she's looking as a man charges straight toward her, while another man dressed in white is holding onto her arms keeping her still as she fights to get away.

What the fuck?

I have one thing on my mind, rip them apart.

I am across the room in seconds and I catch the guy before he can even touch her, throwing him back away from her.

I turn to the guy holding her, the one dressed in white and rip his fingers off her arm.

"Big fucking mistake," I growl at him, my fingers gripping his. I turn them back slowly, watching in fucking glee as he screams, cries and begs for me to let him go.

But I don't, I don't until I hear the popping sound of his bones breaking, then I stop.

I turn around and grab Lee before he can hit me with the fucking chair. I pull his wrist around until he lets go of it.

"What the fuck?" Lee screams at me, I tighten my hand on his throat. "Why are you interfering! This is God's will!" he screams so loudly, spit is flying from his mouth.

I can feel Lynn behind me, watching me but I can't look at her because if I do, I will murder everyone here but there's no fun in that. "Why are you here, Demon? You are a sinner and you have no rights to be in my presence!" he screams once more, his face growing redder by the second.

He is fucking nuts.

I laugh at this pathetic excuse of a man. "I am a sinner, yes, but I am the Grim fucking Reaper." I put my face in front of his, wanting him to look me in my eyes. I can see the fear in his, his hope of getting away flying out of the window. "It's time for me to fucking Reap."

I slam his face into the wall as hard as I can, wanting him to feel all of the pain. I push his face into the wall, dragging it out, I want him to suffer.

I bring him back to me, anger burning me from the inside

out. "But, I'm not going to kill you today." I squeeze his face with all of my might, his eyes frantically searching around the room hoping someone is going to help him. No one will, especially not the fucker lying on the ground moaning over his fucking broken fingers.

"I won't tomorrow, maybe not even ten years from now. No, you are going to suffer, you tried to kidnap *my* daughter. You were going to hurt *my* woman. For that, you are going to live, but you are going to live how I say so and it's not going to be easy. You will feel pain all of your days and no matter what I do to you? It won't ever be enough. It will never be enough but I will make sure that you will feel hell on earth. That I can't fucking wait for."

I smash his face down once more onto the wall, his body hitting the floor, knocked out cold.

I stare down at his lifeless body, sickened by him. How someone can be like this I can't even fucking fathom. But he is no more, his life is over and he can never hurt anyone else.

I turn to face the man who is holding his wounded hand. "I am a prophet, you will be punished for this. She is my wife and you will not interfere," he spouts off to me.

I look to Lynn who is pale as a ghost looking at the man on the ground. "Nah, she's mine." I look at her. "Turn your head, baby." She looks away and I take out my gun pointing it at his dick pulling the trigger.

He is going to be joining Lee in hell.

She looks at me after the gun goes off, ignoring the screams of the man on the ground and runs to me.

I wrap my arms around her, holding her to my chest. "It's all over my girl, I promise," I tell her.

Hours Later

WE ARE LYING IN BED, the TV on in the background both of us not watching it. I'm trying to come to terms with what happened tonight.

Obviously, there was no patient and they used my mom as a ruse.

I close my eyes tightly, lying my head on Tristan's chest, my heart hurting. I was so scared but not for me as much as Michaela. I am so thankful that she wasn't with me tonight.

Everything happened in a whirlwind after Tristan called his MC; minutes later the MC came in and took them away.

I won't ever forget the way they looked at me as they were loaded into the van, they were blaming me for everything. I heard Tristan's words, I know their death isn't going to be soon at all but it will happen and I have that peace in my heart knowing that she is going to be safe.

That is what matters most.

She was born into their world, a world of horrible and corrupt things. It's my job to protect her from that. Now, after eight years of her life, it'll be easier.

We are both free.

Tristan rubs my back, goosebumps following the wake of his fingers. "It's all over, isn't it?" I repeat my thoughts to him.

He lets out a deep breath. "Yeah baby, it's over. You are free, the only ties you had to the cult are gone, over. You can breathe now, angel." With his words, I break down.

I couldn't stop the tears even if I wanted to. I bury my face into the side of his neck and let out the years and years of pain.

Nothing compares to the months of pain when Michaela was almost kidnapped, the sounds of her screams as I ran to her as fast as I could, but it wasn't fast enough to reach her in time. I know those nightmares will never leave me.

Tristan saved her and burrowed his way into our lives, never leaving us. He made our family whole; he gave us a part in our lives that we didn't know that we needed.

But most of all, he's in our hearts. God, I love him so much that it physically hurts me.

I never dreamed that I would have this in my life, I wasn't looking for it. I never expected him and I got used to the fact that I would forever be alone. Tristan let me know that I will never have to walk another step in my life without him, every moment of every day, he is with me.

I think of the way Michaela accidentally called him Daddy and I know in that moment, his life changed. I will never forget the way it almost knocked him on his ass. How since that moment, he was truly hers.

I will never forget how we took Zane into our home and hearts; the way Tristan rocked him all night long when he wasn't feeling well, how he gets up all night long with me to take care of him.

That first night that Tristan came into our lives, he slept on the floor by the bed so we felt safe, he watched over us, protected us to make sure Michaela knew he was there for her and me.

The way he took her on her first date, spoiled her and showed her the way a woman is supposed to be treated. How he reads to her every single night, never misses a game.

The way he treats me, how much he loves me, I feel it deep in my core. With every single world, touch, he shows me how deep his love can go.

I lean up and I smile down at him, I rest my hand on his cheek. "I'm pregnant."

EPILOGUE

MONTHS LATER...

I'M LYING in bed smiling at the ceiling as Tristan and Michaela are having full-blown conversations with my belly.

"Now listen baby, you have to play dolls with me when we get older," Michaela orders to the baby, he or she makes their self known by kicking back at them.

She giggles her sweet giggles, pressing into the spot where the baby kicked. "Daddy loves you, my sweet baby."

Zane decides to make himself known in the conversation by babbling baby talk. Tristan reaches up and snatches him out of the crib lifting him over his head pretending he is an airplane.

"That's the stinkiest airplane I have ever seen." Michaela clamps her nose closed, waving her hand around.

I laugh at her, trying to grab Zane from Tristan who pulls him out of the way. "He's too heavy for you," Tristan informs me for the tenth time.

I roll my eyes, Tristan acts like I'm fragile and with any single weight that I'm going to break any second.

"Tristan I'm fine; he's not that heavy." I try to take him again and he just takes him further out of my grip.

I sit up holding my belly. "Tristan Blane, give me our son," I say in the meanest voice I can muster.

Michaela bursts out laughing, holding her hand over her mouth. "Mom, you sound like Darth Vader."

I grab her foot, lifting it up. "Oh yeah, call me that again!" I say in Darth Vader's voice, tickling her foot. She screams and kicks her leg trying to pull loose, but I hold on tickling her until she screams uncle.

Tristan is watching us both holding baby Zane; happy looks so good on him. On all of us.

It's been months since what happened in Summer's office, but we have had peace in our lives since. It's fucking great, their hands go straight to my stomach once more, both of them obsessed. "I love you guys," I tell them.

Michaela hugs my stomach, Tristan kisses my lips. "I love you too, Momma."

Lynn
Michaela
Eighteen Years Old

"KICK THEIR ASS, BABY!" Tristan screams from the fence below us, Zane who is now ten is standing right beside him cheering his sister on.

Michaela is playing softball and this is her last game before she graduates and let me tell you, this shit is heartbreaking.

She gives her dad a shit-eating grin letting him know that's exactly what she plans on doing.

Our precious baby girl, Trinity is sitting next to me with her nose in a book with the whole world happening around her, oblivious to it all.

I stand up so I can see Michaela. She swings her bat and readies herself to hit the ball.

I hold my breath waiting for her nod to let the pitcher know she is ready. This game is for the USA championship.

Next year she is competing in the Olympics and we are so proud of her. That has been a goal of hers since she was younger and learned what the Olympics were.

Tristan half covers his eyes and leaves enough room so he can peek through his fingers at her. It all happens in slow motion as the ball makes it way toward her, it's deathly silent, no one is breathing.

Whack!

She hits the ball hard and I scream at the top of my lungs running down the bleachers so I can get a closer look as the ball soars toward the back of the field.

She takes off, her friends running along the bases with her. She makes it to second base and is rounding third base when they grab the ball. They throw it toward her and I hold my breath as the runs toward home.

They chase her with the ball, she slides face-first into the home base barely making it before they touch her with the ball.

She flips around on her back, her fist in the air. "Fuck yes!" she screams and I look down at the ground as Tristan glares at her for cursing.

"Going to be the fucking death of me," he mumbles and I pat him on the back knowing that it's a battle that he can't win.

Zane charges out onto the field, dragging her off the ground so he can hug her. They have always been so close.

Zane is a literal mini me of Tristan, their personalities are the same. Trinity is more me than Tristan, but she gets her love of reading apparently from Walker who is an avid reader himself.

We follow him onto the field. "I am so happy for you my girl, you did it." I kiss her cheek, hugging her tight feeling emotional because my baby is grown up and that's hard to believe.

I still think of that small little girl who was absolutely

obsessed with princesses. Tristan takes my place and lifts her off the ground hugging her tight. "I have never been prouder of you, baby girl," he tells her. She closes her eyes and I know his words are affecting her.

He is her world; they are so close even to this day.

She pushes back from him. "Thanks Dad, you pushed me to get through it."

He looks down at the ground but I saw those tears in his eyes. "Yeah well, I love you, baby."

She hugs him again. "I love you too, Dad."

Michaela
Eighteen Years Old

I CLIMB into the playhouse that papa bear had built for me all of those years ago, we spent so many hours in here and he would play with me.

I sit down in the little chair and take one of the dolls that I left here many years ago. The small door opens and Walker walks inside, he pushes his massive frame into one of those little chairs.

"What has you thinking so hard?" he asks me.

I laugh at how ridiculous he looks. "I thought for a long time that my dream was just to play sports but I think I have a new one," I tell him what I have been stewing over.

He sits forward, his elbows on his knees. "Yeah, what's that?"

I purse my lips together, trying to keep my face straight. "A biker of course."

His face shows his shock at my response but I can't hold it in, I burst out laughing. "Sorry, I had to. I do love to ride though, but I am thinking I want to be a surgeon."

His face changes to one of a proud smile. "You can be a

surgeon if you want sweetheart, you can do anything you want to do in life."

My chest warms at his praise, I scoot my little chair over and give him a big hug. "Love you, papa bear."

He tightens his big arms around me. "I love you, princess."

Tristan

"KNOCK KNOCK!" I push open the basement door and try not to cringe at the smell of shit that hits me.

I take in the pitiful sight that is Lee; I gave up torturing him years ago. He just sits in the darkness and his mind has taken over; he lost it years ago.

But not without him seeing Michaela growing up and that he could never have her. He has lived the last ten years of his life in this dark, cold hell.

How fucking fun.

He turns to look at me. "You are going to hell for the way you have kept her from..." His words stop as my bullet hits him in the middle of the forehead.

The last piece of that part of my life is over, death was not meant for him easily. I wanted him to suffer, I want him to be in the jail that he wanted to put my girls in.

I look back one last time at his lifeless body. "Too bad, I should have left you here longer."

I walk upstairs and Trinity runs into my legs. I sweep her up in the air putting her on my hip even though she is a big girl. My wife is leaning against the counter, I press my lips to hers for a brief moment savoring it. "How's my ole lady?" I pat her ass.

"Happy." She gives me her blissful smile, I turn around and look at everyone in the room, my brothers, their women and kids.

Fucking bliss.

"Yeah, me too."

Yes, you guessed it!
Walker, Summer, and Darren is next!

WANT MORE TO READ?
HERE ARE MY OTHER WORKS!
Forever Series

Protecting His Forever

Loving His Forever

Cherishing His Forever

Devil Souls MC Series

Torch

Techy

Butcher

Liam
Kyle, Ryan, Jack Boxset Novella

Grim Sinners MC Series

Lane

Wilder

Travis

Aiden

Derek

Tristan

Grim Sinners MC Originals
Smiley

Maverick

Konrad

Walker (Coming Soon)

This series is under my paranormal pen name:

Teagan Wilde

Raleigh Texas Wolves

Damon
Brantley - Coming Soon

WANT MORE TO READ?

HERE ARE MY OTHER WORKS!

Forever Series
Protecting His Forever
Loving His Forever
Cherishing His Forever

Devil Souls MC Series
Torch
Techy
Butcher
Liam
Kyle, Ryan, Jack Boxset Novella

Grim Sinners MC Series
Lane
Wilder
Travis
Aiden
Derek
Tristan

Grim Sinners MC Originals
Smiley
Maverick
Konrad
Walker (Coming Soon)

This series is under my paranormal pen name:

Teagan Wilde

Raleigh Texas Wolves
Damon
Brantley - Coming Soon

Made in the USA
Coppell, TX
29 March 2022